D1635176

Hostile bid

BY

Helen B. Beveridge.

BEST WISHES.

H. B. Bev.

H B Beveridge

Dedication

to

Kay a much-loved niece.

.

Also by Helen B Beveridge.

Binding Contract

The long Vacation

Give me five minutes more

The Four Poster

Sleeping Partner

The Portrait

Alias

Chapter 1

Belinda looked at her Father and wondered where her good-natured and lovable Father had disappeared to these days and was suddenly anxious, why she did not know. He had been acting strange for some time now, rapid mood swings and no appetite, forgetful and downright hostile at times with her. She dare not think far less say the word dementia. As for asking her Father to see a doctor she kept putting off the suggestion, as she knew he would probably explode. It was an uneasy situation and she felt responsible for his welfare since her mother was no longer with them.

Belinda's Mother had died a few years ago and as the only child she had taken over the running of the large rambling house, given up her flat and moved in to look after her Father who was completely hopeless on his own. She had given up the career she had hoped to achieve without a second thought and not out of a sense of duty. There had only ever been one drawback, she knew her Father had wanted a son to carry on the family business and in that respect she was a disappointment to him and yet he would always deny the fact. Apart from that they got along really well or had done until some months ago.

"Why not have a day off, you worked all week-end again and you look tired. We could go for a drive or something, get you to relax a bit I am sure you are stressed out."

"What a load of rubbish you come out with these days Belle. Tired, relax, you treat me like an old man and I am in my prime as for stress there is no such thing. Work is what I know work is what I do and yes, work is my whole life since your Mother died. We started with nothing and built up the business, which is thriving by the way but you cannot afford to take your eye off the ball for a second or you are done for business these days is cut-throat. Harcourt Services is all I have and all I live for these days."

"Even managing directors take a break and you have Uncle Giles to keep things ticking over so you can afford to take a break. You haven't taken one day off since Mum died and that is four years ago, that can't be good for you everyone needs a break now and again even Peter Harcourt."

"Since your Mother died God bless her, it has been work that has kept me going, nothing else." "Thank you very much Dad that makes me feel so much better, now I know exactly what I mean to you." Belinda retorted feeling very hurt indeed by his remarks.

CHAPTER 2

"Oh! For god's sake don't bring that up again I am sick of it and I am in no mood to argue about genders yet again. Get me my coat it is time I was off I have a business to run."

"At least eat some breakfast before you go, it is still early so you have plenty of time."

"Don't really have time Belle in any case I am not hungry. I will get something later at the office if I feel like it. See you this evening might be a bit late though a lot of catching up to do."

"Catching up what do you mean, the past few months you have even gone in on the Sunday. Let me come with you I am sure I can help ease the load a bit if only you would let me, there are many things I could do to ease the burden."

"I haven't time for this conversation and I want you kept out of the business how often must you be told."

Belle watched him drive away and shrugged her shoulders. I wish Mum were here she was thinking, she would sort him out and find out what was wrong, she could always get round him no matter what mood he was in. She cleared up the uneaten food and decided she would spend the morning weeding the garden then do some

painting in the afternoon but she was
not happy, she knew there was
something very amiss but what?

CHAPTER 3

Nine in the evening and still no sign of her Father and the evening meal was ruined. This was not good enough so Belle rang the office and allowed it to ring and ring for some considerable time determined she would get an answer.

Finally her Father lifted the receiver. "I will be home soon what is all the fuss about."

"This has got to stop Dad you are going to kill yourself, is the business in trouble is that why you are not your usual self? I know something is very wrong I'm not stupid."

"Don't talk rubbish the business is thriving and the order book is overflowing, Harcourt Services is booming. We need to expand that is why I am working so late drawing up the plans and organising the finance. I grabbed a sandwich here so eat by yourself tonight, I will see you in the morning."

Belle was really angry why the need to expand? They had a large house and could pay all the bills that landed on their doorstep, so why slave away twenty-four hours every day just to expand and in the process end up in an early grave. She heard him come home at three in the morning and was furious with him. She was fast losing patience with his sullen behaviour.

Belle tackled him at breakfast next morning. "You cannot keep this up, you will end up in an early grave and where will Harcourt Services be then and also what happens to me or don't you care."

"I am doing this for you Belle, I know you think I would rather have had a son but believe it or not I love you very much indeed just as much as any son."

"You are not doing this for me so don't dare say that, I don't want loads of money I just want us to have some life together, but you are never away from that lousy office. I have tried many times to join you at the company and help to spread the load but you steadfastly refuse and I know it is because I am female what other reason can there be. I could help a great deal if you would only give me the opportunity."

"I will not listen to anymore of this garbage, your thinking is all warped about being female. I will tell you for the last time I love you and appreciate all you do for me especially since your Mother died. I know you gave up a great deal to come and look after me. As for Harcourt's you will never ever work there so you can forget about that, it will never happen as long as I am alive, end of discussion. I will see you tonight but I don't know at what time so have dinner on your own."

Belle walked away, it was like talking to a brick wall and she could see no valid reason against joining her Father in the business. At twenty-six she was a responsible adult and thought she could bring a great deal to the business, she did have a few talents but all she was fit for was housekeeping and having babies, her Father obviously was living in Victorian times, she vowed not to broach the subject ever again as it hurt to be constantly rebuffed.

CHAPTER 4

Two weeks later her Father walked through the door at 10pm. Threw his coat and briefcase on the floor then slumped into the nearest chair.

"Get me a brandy Belle on second thoughts make it a double. I'm in trouble, real trouble this time and it's going to be touch and go, I will need all my wits about me this time if I am to survive."

Belle was at his side immediately. "What's wrong, are you ill?"

"No I'm not ill it's Harcourt Services my life's work that is in trouble. The business has been approached with a view to a take-over and the man behind it is utterly ruthless."

"I thought the business was booming that was what you said, I don't understand."

"Being a successful business makes us a target for a take-over which in reality is really asset stripping. This man Dawson is trying to buy up all the shares and make a hostile bid for the company. He has a reputation for getting what he wants but not this time. Together Giles and I will fight him off, we have an emergency board meeting next week and we will send him away with a flea in his ear, he will not tackle us again I will make bloody sure of that."

"Why so worried then, surely the board meeting is just a formality."

"You never know with these type of meetings and Dawson has a huge reputation, he has taken over many businesses all in the same way and never failed to win."

Belle did not like the sound of this man Dawson; there were too many men like him waiting for the chance to pounce and steal all the profits that other people had worked years to accrue. At least it was not a real worry Dad had Uncle Giles to back him up and this pariah could never win, as he would never obtain the required shares. Uncle Giles had thirty and Dad had forty-eight so this Dawson character would be thwarted this time round.

"Not to worry Dad you and Uncle Giles are sitting pretty with your combined shares he is on a hiding to nothing this time."

"As you say Belle he is fighting a losing battle with Harcourt Services and no mistake, I can't wait to see him off."

Hostile bid

During the night Belle heard her Dad walking the floor of his bedroom and cursed this man Dawson for upsetting her Father. As if he didn't have enough to worry about with all his expansion plans, now he had to fight a hostile bid. That scavenger Dawson was a rat, thank goodness he would be seen off very quickly.

Chapter 5

Belle insisted on accompanying her Father the day of the board meeting, it was her way of showing support even though he did not need it. She sat in his office reading a book and wishing she could work here with her Father. There were many talents she could bring to the business if only her Father would relent. She was not the least bit worried about this board meeting it was just a formality and this Dawson character would soon be leaving with his tail between his legs, unsuccessful this time round.

The meeting was much shorter than she expected and her Father appeared very quickly. But immediately he walked into the office and she saw his face she knew the meeting had gone against him, but how was that possible?

"Sit down Dad before you fall down, I will get you a drink."

"I don't want anything Belle, I am finished and would you believe it my own brother voted against me. As if that wasn't enough to make matters worse he has actually sold his shares to that scurrilous Dawson. Believe it or not he now has control of Harcourt Services and I am of no further use, redundant, on the scrap heap at my age I wish they had just shot me in there and been done with it."

"We can still fight, can't we?"

"Nothing to fight with Belle and I don't have the will or the energy to go on I am so tired and completely worn out. To tell the truth this has completely finished me, I have lost the company your Mother and I spent our lives building and it is all down to pure greed. I never thought for a second Giles my own brother would stab me in the back like this."

"Forget Uncle Giles he is a traitor and don't dare say you are finished you have many years in front of you. Maybe we can sell your shares to this Dawson vulture and start up a new company. You and I could go into competition and show him he has won nothing of value, you have all the contacts and we will do it together just you and I. We can do this Dad I know we can, you and I are a force to be reckoned with don't you think?"

Peter Harcourt didn't even smile at the idea. "I have built up this company from nothing and am too old to start again. Since your Mother died the company was all I had left. Now I have had that taken away from me and in the most humiliating way, they even stripped me of what little dignity I had left. They have made sure I have been left with absolutely nothing, I tell you Belle I really am finished this time. I stand before you now a broken man."

"You still have me, what about me Dad?"

"Sorry Belle, I love you very much you know that but a man must have an interest apart from family and that has just been taken away from me. I am left with absolutely nothing. A complete waste of space."

"So I mean nothing to you, I always knew you would have preferred a son but you would never admit it, at least now I know where I really stand." Belle retorted feeling deeply hurt and very upset.

Peter simply shrugged his shoulders. "I have no fight left in me to argue that old chestnut, you can think what you bloody wish I need to get out of this infernal place." He picked up his coat and walked out of the office.

"Dad wait for me I am coming with you."

He ignored her call and was gone; he walked away like an old man, shoulders hunched, head bowed and Belle wanted to weep at the way he had been treated.

She sat at her Father's desk and wondered how after all her twenty-six years it always came down to the same argument that she should have been male and she had been a huge disappointment to him and she felt the tears sting.

"Where is Peter?" Uncle Giles asked as he entered the office.

"How could you sell Dad out like that Uncle Giles?" Belle's eyes were blazing with real anger.

"Belle darling I did what was best for Harcourt Services and your Father. Peter lost his grip a very long time ago, four years to be exact he has never been the same since your Mother died."

"No that is bloody rubbish, you did what was best for Giles Harcourt and I will never forgive you. Voting against him was bad enough but selling your shares was downright brutal and you didn't even warn him in advance, just pulled the rug out from under him and humiliated him publicly."

"You don't know the circumstances and I am not about to enlighten you I don't have the time, I must find Peter. Suffice to say Mark Dawson will drag this company into the twenty-first century and make it highly successful again, now I really must find Peter it is important he understands I did it for him."

"The order book is full and Dad was planning an expansion so I don't believe you. You sold out your own brother for thirty pieces of silver, how could you stoop so low and still live with yourself?"

Giles glared at Belle but decided to hold his tongue, now was not the time for home truths and he was desperate to find his brother and explain his actions today had been for the best.

"If Mark Dawson is such a financial genius why sell your shares now and not wait until he expands the company. Look at the money you could pocket then"

"I am only three years younger than your Father. It is time to get out of harness and enjoy the pleasures of life. I am too old to be working all hours of the day and night. To be honest I have had enough of Harcourt Services."

"You working all hours don't make me laugh. You barely lifted a finger and sat on your fat posterior and lined your pockets over Dad's sweat. You are disgusting Uncle Giles and you are a bloody traitor."

"Once the dust has settled and you have calmed down I will explain a few facts to you, then you will understand I did what was best for my brother and the business and without doubt you will take back the names you have called me. Now I really must find Peter." Giles voice was very quiet.

"Mark Dawson will find out very quickly he does not have it all his own way. No doubt it is all about asset stripping. Dad still has forty-eight percent of this company and he will never sell." Belle stood up and as she walked towards the door she turned round.

"I no longer have an Uncle Giles, you are a traitor of the worst kind who sold his brother out for money and out of pure greed and you chose to do it in the most diabolical manner. I will never ever speak to you again and you are no longer welcome at the house."

Belle made her way home and decided this was the saddest day of her life. Little did she know more sadness was to come her way?

Chapter 6

Her Father was not at home and she wondered where he was, she hoped he would not do something silly and finish himself off and she shuddered at the very thought.

She prepared the evening meal and waited for him to come home but he never did. She received a call from the hospital; her Father had taken a massive heart attack and crashed the car. There was little they could do for him and she was advised to come quickly.

Belle sat by the bed and held his hand.

"I do love you and I never ever wished for a boy that is the truth." He whispered.

She kissed him and held on to his hand with tears in her eyes. "We will start a new life together when you get better. It will be you and I against the world just like it was after Mum died, we will show them all we are made of stern stuff we Harcourt's."

"You and I both know I am not going to make it out of here but I needed to wait to speak to you. Your Mother is here waiting for me that makes me very happy and I want to be with her. Look after yourself find a man who truly loves you and have children. The shares are yours, do what you wish with them they are of no consequence now, all I want now is for you to be happy and I am truly sorry. I hope in time you will forgive me but I really thought I was doing the right thing at the time."

Peter closed his eyes and Belle was relieved he had fallen asleep, as he looked so tired. She sat for a while watching him sleep and was still holding his hand when the nurse came in and said he had passed away peacefully.

Belle was devastated and very angry so immediately looked for someone to blame; she did not need to look very far. Uncle Giles and this vulture Mark Dawson, she had given her Uncle Giles a few home truths and although she had never met this Mark Dawson she promised herself he would be told in no uncertain terms he was responsible for her Father's death the first opportunity she got. The one consolation being her Father had not died alone.

CHAPTER 7

Belle did not sleep that night but wandered around the house hoping her Father would walk through the door at any minute but she knew that would never happen. She went into his bedroom and sat on his bed even turned it down, then took his pyjamas from under the pillow all ready and waiting for him.

Very early next morning Belle went to her Father's office to collect his personal effects. When she opened the door a strange man was sitting at the desk and she simply erupted.

"Who are you? You have no right to be in here, I suggest you leave now before I throw you out."

"I am Mark Dawson what can I do for you?" Mark asked as he stood up.

"You did not waste any time did you. You are a vulture picking over my Father's bones have you no decency?"

"Calm down now, whose bones did you say I was picking over"?

"I am Belinda Harcourt my Father is Peter Harcourt founder of Harcourt Services. You humiliated and finished him yesterday with the help of Uncle Giles, I hope you are really proud of yourself."

"Just a moment, what do you mean by finished? I have never finished anyone in my entire life." Mark declared looking very angry.

"You took away the only thing he lived for and now you are busy asset stripping and will soon disappear back under the stone you crawled out from under. I have met rogues like you before but you will find I am not so easy to dismiss. I have my Father's shares in this company and you will find you have started world war three you unscrupulous lout. Now get out of this office it is mine not yours and how dare you sit in my Father's chair, you are not fit to even lick his boots you stinking degenerate."

Mark stood staring at Belle unable to believe she had just called him an unscrupulous lout. No one had ever dared to speak to him like that, he valued his reputation above all else and to be called degenerate, well he had had enough and he was extremely angry.

"I dear lady have a controlling interest in this company and if anyone leaves it will be you. I will also never tolerate anyone calling me a degenerate. Do you even know the meaning of the word?"

"Yes indeed I do know exactly what it means and I am quite happy to spell it out for you. You are debased, immoral, debauched, corrupt and downright greedy. Now you also know what it means, does that satisfy you?"

Mark was speechless he walked around her and left the room in a hurry.

Belle occupied her Father's chair and began to go though all the drawers in his desk. Suddenly the door opened and Mark Dawson entered accompanied by two security guards.

"Get this deranged woman off these premises and make sure she does not come back."

Belle smiled. "Hello Sam what do you think of your new boss, not much I bet. You will soon be out of a job when he strips the place bare."

Sam's face was crimson. "I cannot throw this lady out she is the boss's daughter."

"I am your boss now and you will follow my orders or you will be out on your ear pronto just like this demented woman."

Sam saw by his face Mr. Dawson was about ready to explode and was unsure what he should do.

"If my Father were here would you be throwing him out?" Belle enquired.

"Of course not but you are not your Father and you cannot come in here throwing your weight about whenever you feel like it." Mark met her eyes and refused to look away.

"Thanks to you my Father died last night and now I have his shares, just you try and throw me out you murdering swine. I will create such a commotion you will run a bloody mile."

Mark's face fell and he felt really bad. "I'm so sorry you have my condolences. If there is anything I can do you only have to ask"?

"You have already done your worst, you sent him to his grave yesterday and I will see you in hell before I am finished and you can take that as a promise, not a warning."

Mark dismissed the guards.

"I am truly sorry he was a good man." Sam said as he left.

"Why did you not say you had lost your Father?" Mark asked accusingly.

26

"It would have made no difference to a filthy reprobate like you."

"Listen to me young lady. I have had just about as much as I can take with your foul accusations, has anyone told you that you have a mouth like a sewer. The board decided what was to be done not I and I have no intentions of asset stripping either. I will bring this company into the twenty-first century and make it a vibrant business again. I had nothing against your Father but business is business."

"Business stinks then and so do you." Belle roared.

Mark was desperately trying to control his temper. This woman was a wild cat. "We must sort all this out but this is neither the time nor the place. I suggest we meet again after the funeral and try to come to some agreement. In the meantime you can avail yourself of this office until then"

"Thanks for nothing you scumbag, you know what you can do with your lousy office and I hope it hurts like hell."

"Did your Father not teach you some manners? I would also hate to see the dictionary you use."

"My Father could make a thousand of you, you creep. Unlike you he was an honourable man not a Judas or a sneak. As for the dictionary I use there are no words vile enough in it to describe someone such as you."

"There is no talking to you is there?" Mark commented as he left the room. He walked down the corridor and punched the wall at one point. What on earth had he got mixed up in this time? He was wishing he had never heard of Harcourt Services.

Chapter 8

Belle emptied all the drawers and threw everything in a box; she would go through the lot when she got home the faster she was out of here the better the company was simply vile. She lifted her Mother's portrait off the desk and suddenly her anger evaporated and she felt very much alone and for the first time since her Father died she began to cry. Once she started she could not stop and the tears just streamed down her face.

Mark Dawson seemed to appear from nowhere. He moved towards her and put his hand on her shoulder and it made her cry all the more. He was the sworn enemy and she did not want sympathy from him. Next thing she knew she had her face buried in his jacket and it felt so comforting.

"If you are finished here for the moment I will take you home."

Belle sat up straight and wiped her eyes. "I would not accept help from you if you were the last man on earth. I will see myself home you greedy horrible distasteful monster." She stood up, lifted the box and marched out the door still crying. She leaned against the wall in the corridor then slid down to the floor the tears streaming down her face.

Mark helped her up. "I will take you home now, no more arguments."

He drove her home and settled her in a chair then went and made coffee. "Drink this it will make you feel better."

"Nothing will make me feel better I just want my Father back." Belle began to cry again.

"Is there someone who can stay with you?"

"No there was just Dad and I." She sobbed even harder.

"Then I will stay with you until you feel better."

Belle lay on the sofa and finally cried herself to sleep. Mark put a blanket over her and took his leave. He was worried about her but there was nothing he could do. He remembered when his Father had died and he thought his world had come to an end.

Given time Belinda Harcourt would survive and be ready to fight the good fight again. My goodness what a tongue she had on her, very beautiful, very much a lady until she opened her mouth and her words never missed their mark.

Spirit, she had enough spirit for a dozen women and secretly he admired that. She would be up on her feet again very soon and woe betides whoever got on her wrong side, he just hoped it would not be himself.

Belle woke up and it was dark outside she must have slept for a good few hours. Her face grew hot as she remembered crying on Mark Dawson's shoulder. A complete stranger and a despicable enemy whom she was at war with and intended to see him destroyed like he had destroyed her beloved Father. "I will sort him out Dad don't you fret." She said to his photograph.

The funeral was a week later and there were many mourners wishing to pay their last respects, which pleased Belle enormously it seemed her Father had been well thought of in the business world. Mark Dawson was there and she avoided him like the plague until he finally cornered her.

"You have my condolences, we must have that talk sometime soon."

Uncle Giles approached her but she spurned him, it was too late for him to feel sorry for what he had done. She walked away from them both her head held high as they both disgusted her, a right greedy pair.

The house was not the same without her parents it was much too quiet, this was a family house but they were all gone except her and she wanted to cry again. She put the box with her father's papers on the table but as soon as she lifted the lid she started to cry again. Leave it for another day she told herself she had a lifetime to go through it.

The solicitor called the next day to read her Father's will. As expected everything had been left to Belle and Peter had stressed that he had been very proud of his daughter. Better than a hundred sons he had written, a very beloved and loyal daughter a true blessing indeed.

It came as a surprise when she was informed there was no money after all the debt had been cleared. Dad had told her the business was thriving. Oh! Of course he must have spent the money on his expansion plans that would not come cheap would it?

"The house is safe so you will always have a roof over your head." The solicitor informed her.

Belle was unconcerned about the lack of money all she could think of was her Father's words, better than a hundred sons. His words made her very happy and now she could put that thought out of her mind once and for all, it made her feel very good, as for being loyal Dawson would soon find out to his cost what loyalty was all about, she would make sure of that if it was the last thing she did.

Chapter 9

A week later Mark Dawson rang and asked her to come to the office. "We must get things settled." He explained.

"I will sort things out in my own time not yours, no doubt you are keen to do business when I am at a low ebb and take advantage of the situation well think again." Belle put the phone down on the greedy man.

Mark was furious when she hung up on him. The woman was a wild cat no mistake about it and he was at the receiving end. He was getting mighty tired of all the insults she threw at him without just cause and yet there was something about her that drew him to her. "Yes, like a spider to its web." He said aloud. "But I am not a foolish man she can spin her web but she will never entice me."

Mark had his solicitor send her a letter requesting a meeting at a time suitable to her. He did not require waiting long for her answer.

Mr. Greedy Guts, I see you cannot keep your avarice in check, shame on you. As I said re the phone call I will meet you to discuss matters as and when it suits me. You may have had it easy with all the other companies you filched but you will find I am a very different proposition altogether. I will do the dictating this time not you and don't you forget it.

Belinda Harcourt.

Of all the insolence, Mark tore the letter up and put it in the bin. So what she had 48% but he was in the driving seat with 51% and intended to get more, it would make no difference to making Harcourt Services a viable business again and that was what he intended. No wild cat would stop him and she would find that out before long, she had started a war she could never win and her facts were all wrong anyway.

Two months later Belle realised she had very little money left. Better get all the loose ends tied up she thought and called Harcourt Services and agreed on a meeting the next day. She took particular care in how she dressed and wished to look very efficient and used to high-powered meetings.

"Take a seat Miss Harcourt again I am sorry for your loss."

"Thank you."

"Let us get down to the business in hand. Have you spoken with your Father's solicitor?"

"Yes of course."

"Then you will be aware that Harcourt Services was in dire straits until I came on board and I intend to stop the rot. I will buy your shares and give you a good price which under the circumstances is an exceptionally good offer."

Belle stared at him and did not avert her eyes until it was he who finally looked away.

"My father was hardly cold in his grave when you were already picking over his bones. Yes, I was correct the first day I met you, you really are a bloody vulture."

"We will have less of the name calling Miss Harcourt I have had more than enough of that from you and I warn you now I will take no more of it. I had nothing against your Father and this is purely business." Mark's face was red with anger.

"I was not sure what I would do with the shares before I came in here. Now I know I will keep them just to make life as difficult as possible for you and your cronies."

"Sorry to disappoint you but it will make no difference to my plans for Harcourt Services whether I own your shares or not. I will make a success of Harcourt's whether you like it or not."

"Harcourt Services was and is a thriving company so all you are interested in is asset stripping as always. My shares will be worthless in a few weeks once you have stripped the company totally bare but that is no concern to me I will keep my shares and be damned."

"As a matter of fact young lady this business is on its knees and I intend to rejuvenate it and make it second to none. Look can we begin again, we seem to have got off on the wrong foot from day one and we have both made false assumptions."

Belle stood up. "My first assumption of you Mr Dawson was the correct one. You murdered my Father with the help of Uncle Giles and you enticed him to sell his shares to you so you would have a controlling interest. Bully for you, I take my hat off to you a real enterprising rat if I may say so. As for enticing me to sell you will have to think again as it will never happen as long as I bloody live and I intend to make your rotten little life a misery in every way that I can. You are also a bloody liar and you must take me for a fool. The business is booming and the order book is full and I heard that straight from the horse's mouth so you can stop all your blatant lies."

Mark began to say something but could only watch as she stormed out the office and although he was very angry he had to admit she had the looks and spirit to send a man over the edge. Her dark brown hair piled up on her head and he wondered what it was like hanging loose down her back. Her figure, well it was perfect and she moved so gracefully and when she was angry her green eyes were like flashing fires, a beautiful sight. She should have red hair he decided to match her temper. She definitely had a lot going for her any man would be proud to make her his partner thankfully not I. Work is my only priority and Miss Harcourt was going to give him a fight that he did not want and one she could never hope to win and yet there was something he could not put his finger on. Having said that he had to admit a great admiration for her loyalty and tenacity.

Belle was seething with rage as she left the building. He thought all he had to do was offer her money and she would be eternally grateful for the few crumbs he deigned to toss in her direction. She would make his life hell if she could and to do that she must retain the shares at all cost, she was more than ready for the fight ahead just bring it on.

CHAPTER 10

Belle suddenly found she had no money
left and needed to find work quickly.
She had studied art at the university but
when her Mother died her Father
assumed she would move back home
and look after him, which she did
without even one regret.

Now she was on her own with a large
house, some shares in a so-called run-
down company the liar that he was and
no money. She could not bring herself
to sell the house; she had been born
there. There was no way she would sell
her shares to that abominable man, he
had everything he wanted on a plate
but he would never get his filthy hands
on her shares, it would be over her dead
body.

Belle began to look at all the vacancies
and eventually found what she thought
was the right vacancy for her talents.
An advertising agency that appreciated
her work and when they found out she
was gifted in photography and also an
artist they took her on immediately.

Belle worked very hard and finally after
a few months had one or two accounts.
She did not really enjoy the work but
she needed the money and it was well
paid. Her experience in entertaining her
Father's clients made it possible for her
to wine and dine the agency clients

successfully and soon she had a good many more accounts and they promoted her to a much higher level.

She was pleased she had made a life for herself but she could not say she was happy. Something was missing and she knew it was important to her. She missed her Father but she wanted to know what it was to be loved and to return that love. To be as one with the man she gave herself to and to bear his children if possible, but she didn't think it would ever happen all the men she met were lacking in many respects.

She had been asked out by many of her male colleagues and clients but had always refused. She was a romantic at heart and believed she would meet the perfect man and sparks would fly immediately as soon as their eyes met, love at first sight. A load of stupid rubbish she chided herself. The only sparks recently were with that abhorrent man Mark Dawson and he was her sworn enemy.

He certainly had the looks, bright blue eyes and blonde hair a straight nose and well formed lips; he also had a dimple, which was really cute. A hunky physique and up to the eyeballs in charm, he also knew how to dress well and his ties were always perfect with the suit he wore. Pity he was a bloody rogue, lovely outside but rotten through and through on the inside, yes a really corrupt man. What he had done to her Father had been really brutal and she would never forgive him, she was determined to get her revenge one way or another even if she required playing dirty just like him.

Chapter 11

Belle received a letter from Dawson's solicitor offering her a huge sum of money for her shares and it infuriated her, the rat was intent on getting what he wanted but she was just as intent on keeping her shares although they meant absolutely nothing to her but anything was permissible to thwart greedy guts.

She wrote back to Dawson at Harcourt Services marking it personal.

Dear Greedy Guts, I see you are running true to form, your greed is astounding and you can offer me the whole bloody world but you will never lay your filthy hands on my shares. You have the looks and the charm but that is on the outside, inside you are an unprincipled lout a vulture and a downright degenerate. Your only thought is accruing money and you don't care how low you have to stoop to get it. Well I will spell it out for you one last time you will never ever have my shares and I will see you in hell before I am finished you scumbag."

Belinda Harcourt.

Mark was busy trying to turn the company round; he was working eighteen-hour days and was extremely tired at the end of each day. He was however beginning to see an improvement and he was delighted. What he wanted next was all the shares in the company, he had fifty-one and Belinda Harcourt had forty-eight. He would find out who had the rest and buy them out. For some obscure reason he kept thinking about Belinda Harcourt, probably because she had spirit, which he tended to admire in people.

He received the letter from her to say she would never sell and it made him incandescent with the slurs on his reputation. He was not about to let it go this time, if she wanted a war he would willingly oblige. He wrote back in his own hand and informed her in no uncertain terms if she kept up with her assassination of his character he would see her in court.

When Belle received Mark's letter she tore it up after reading it. She did not think he would go to court it would only make him look exactly what he was a scavenger in the business world. She wrote back and told him it was just sour grapes because he could not get his hands on her shares. She also reiterated he was more or less scum and she would welcome telling all and sundry in court just how his good looks concealed a very dishonourable man. She did not have to wait long for his reply.

Belle received a solicitor's letter demanding she retract all her slanderous remarks, to this end a meeting is arranged between Mark Dawson and Belinda Harcourt in the solicitor's office. It is advisable you bring your own representative.

She realised maybe she had gone a bit too far this time and probably she was in real trouble but she did not care. The way she felt at this precise moment she wished she was a man and she would challenge him to a real fisticuffs, she desperately wanted to give him a real bloody nose.

Mark Dawson was sitting in his solicitor's office awaiting Belinda Harcourt and she was late which infuriated him. He had better things to do than sit around waiting for her. He wanted to see her eating humble pie, the sooner the better then the matter would be closed.

Belle walked into the office ten minutes late and did not even apologise for her lateness. Yet Mark was thrilled to see her, he had forgotten just how beautiful and fascinating she was.

"Have you not brought your representative with you Miss Harcourt?" Mr Benton enquired.

"I don't need anyone." Belle stated as she sat down next to Mark Dawson.

"I am assuming then you are willing to retract all the slanderous remarks you have made concerning my client Mr Mark Dawson." Mr Belton declared.

"You assume wrong I stick by what I have said." Belle said defiantly.

"It is court then." Belton replied quietly. "You do realise how much this will cost you. We will take you for every penny you own."

Belle laughed. "I have no money only a monthly salary. You can't get blood out of a stone, Mr Dawson will tell you that as I am sure he has tried many times."

Belton frowned "I believe you own an Edwardian house and shares. We can take all that from you Miss Harcourt in lieu of actual money."

Belle got really frightened, she had not thought about the house or the shares.

"That will not be necessary if Miss Harcourt gives me an apology here and now and agrees to stop the slanderous remarks we will let it go at that." Mark said swiftly, he did not want it to go this far but he had to stop her crucifying him and he valued his good name.

Belle was surprised; he had the chance to get her shares and her house yet here he was giving her a way out of this mess. Could she be wrong about this man? No, he just had his own agenda as usual.

She swallowed hard stood up and faced Mark. "I am sorry if my anger loosened my tongue and I called you vile names. All I can say is it was down to grief over losing my Father so suddenly. I will not repeat any slanderous remarks in the future you have my word on that and I apologise without reservation."

Mark stood up and smiled at Belle and it took her breath away. He put his hand out and Belle had to shake it and it put a shiver down her spine. "I accept your apology Miss Harcourt and hope we can be friends in the future."

"That is so very kind of you, thank you for being so generous." Belle quickly withdrew her hand from his. "If that is all I will bid you both good day." She walked out the door head held high.

When Belle got outside she was furious. Friends not bloody likely, you can't be friends with a man like that she said to herself. She had swallowed her pride so she could keep the house and the all-important shares but it had been most humiliating. The words had just about choked her having to bow down to that rat. She had lost this battle but the war was not over just yet and she still had the all-important shares to fight with.

Chapter 12

When Belle reached home she decided anger was going to destroy her not Dawson as he held all the top cards bar one. Know your enemy so she went on the Internet and typed in his name. She got quite a shock, it seemed Dawson was a millionaire three times over. His companies were very diverse and all were profitable. He took over ailing firms and turned them round. He was unmarried and was one of the most eligible bachelors around often photographed with top models and actresses. He donated thousands every year to charity a well-respected man in the business world. Yes, he covered up his dirty dealings really well and put up a good front, but she intended to bring him down come what may and show the world the real man underneath.

She realised she had had a lucky escape; he of all people would not tolerate the names she had called him. So what if he was a pillar of society it was all show as he covered his tracks very well indeed. She still wanted retribution for taking everything from her Father but how could it be done? Every company he owned was totally his except Harcourt's and she knew it would stick in his throat she had forty-eight percent of it. If she could find other shareholders and buy them out she would be a worthy opponent for such as him and at any future meetings she would thwart him at each and every turn. She felt really optimistic now she

H B Beveridge

had a plan in mind. "I am not beaten yet Dad afterall I am a Harcourt." She said to the photograph on the table.

CHAPTER 13

Monday morning again and it was the usual staff meeting at the agency.

"We have a new potential client, a very distinguished one at that. If we do well we may get all his business and it is worth a great deal of money." Bertram said as he looked around.

Belle hoped Bertram would choose her, although she was fairly new to the agency she had worked hard and had more than proved herself.

"I want each of you to draw up a campaign and have them on my desk by the end of the week. I will choose the best presentation and award the new account to that person and there is a huge bonus for the right person so get to it and make it superlative."

"What is the product?" Bob asked.

"Patent medicines and all that goes with chemist shops now get on with it and remember this client is very important and I want him on our books so excellence is the byword for this client. There is a great deal depending on this one."

Belle was elated this one was right up her street, her Father's business had been supplying chemist shops and maybe she had a head start. A bonus would be very acceptable at this precise time and she could buy more shares and thwart Mr. Greedy Guts.

For the rest of the week they were all busy setting up presentations for the campaign and for once they were all keeping things close to their chests and there was no swapping of ideas for this one.

At the end of the week Belle handed in her presentation ideas to Bertram along with the others and hoped she would win. She would then have the money to buy out other shareholders and be a real match for Mark Dawson and with luck maybe even finish him. This was what kept her going these lonely days, in fact this is what she really lived for the downfall of her sworn enemy. She wanted to see him on his knees and realise he had met his match and beg for mercy which he would never get and her Father would then rest in peace.

Monday morning at the staff meeting everyone was holding his or her breath to see who the winner would be.

Bertram coughed as he opened the file. "I won't keep you on tenterhooks, Bob is the winner I liked his old style campaign and it is well thought out back to the alchemist era. We will put it to the client on Wednesday. Belle I thought your campaign was brilliant but much too modern, better luck next time."

Belle smiled and congratulated Bob. He had been in the business ten years so she had no hard feelings towards him; the better man won this time so she would need to wait another day to finish Dawson, but she was patient and time was on her side.

Wednesday morning Bob and Bertram left to meet the client and all the talk was how big the bonus would be for Bob.

"Do we know who the client is?" Belle asked.

"No but whoever he is he is big business and the bonus will be enormous, I wish Bertram had chosen me." Paul replied.

Bertram and Bob were back very soon and one look at their faces told all and sundry the client was not impressed.

"Come into the office Belle." Bertram commanded.

"Sit down and listen, the client thought Bob's presentation was dull and very old-fashioned so I got it very wrong. He wants something more modern and up to date so I have set up a meeting for Friday and you will show him what your ideas are."

"Thank you." Belle replied just a little bit excited, maybe she would have the money to buy extra shares afterall.

"It is of the utmost importance we sell your campaign to him as it means a great deal to this agency. I want you to dress up for the meeting and use your charming smile a great deal. This man is very hard to please and we must accommodate him at all costs."

"I will do my best."

"Take today and tomorrow to finalise your presentation, I will leave all the talking to you but make it good as I said before we need him onboard."

Belle took her work home where she could work in peace and quiet. She worked hard and by Thursday evening she was satisfied she could do no better. She had a very modern approach and had Harcourt's in mind all the time she was working on it.

Friday morning she arrived at the office and Bertram was waiting for her.

"The traffic is heavy so we will leave now, being late is not an option especially with this very important client."

"I am ready and waiting." Belle replied with a broad smile, she had a good feeling about this campaign and knew it was excellent.

They were early when they arrived at the hotel and were directed to the suite occupied by the client.

Belle set up all her equipment and pinned her drawings on the board. She wasn't nervous as she had done this many times before and she had confidence her work would pass muster.

"You have changed a few things." Bertram commented as he looked at her drawings.

"Yes, but I think I have improved them"

"I agree much better than before, you have worked really hard on this one thank you."

Bertram smiled, he had great faith in Belle and so far she had never let him down and this campaign was top-notch. She was wearing an emerald two-piece that hugged her figure and emphasised the green of her eyes. Her hair was loose but held away from her face with

a fancy clasp. She oozed sex appeal and
yet seemed totally unaware of the fact.
He prayed her looks alone would clinch
the deal, as this was make or break
time for the business and if they were
not successful the business would fold.

CHAPTER 14

Belle was looking out the window at the superb view. "You can see the whole of London from here."

"Yes indeed, it is a marvellous sight don't you think?"

Belle knew the voice only too well and her face was flushed as she turned round to face greedy-guts.

"May I introduce you, this is Belinda Harcourt one of our top people." Bertram said as he shook hands.

"We have met." Mark replied as he took in her appearance. "It is indeed a pleasure to see you again Miss Harcourt and under these circumstances. Yes, a most pleasant surprise."

Belle wanted to say it was no pleasure for her but a real nasty shock, but she kept her anger in check and gave him a smile.

"If you are ready we will run through the campaign we have lined up for you Mr Dawson, business is business as they say."

"I hope it is better than the last attempt I was most disappointed." Mark remarked as he sat down.

Bertram sensed an atmosphere in the air and was not sure where it was coming from. "I apologise for the first campaign we got it horrible wrong that is why I have put my very best artist on this one. I am sure you will be delighted."

Belle wanted out of the room as quickly as possible, there was something about this man that intimidated her and she detested the feeling, she was as good as him, no she was much better as she had morals unlike him.

"Look time is money can we skip the chit chat and get on with the presentation or we will be here all day."

Bertram gave her a huge scowl, which she totally ignored and proceeded to run through the presentation at an alarming rate and she prayed Dawson would hate the campaign, as she wanted out of here and soon before she ignited.

"This is most interesting, I missed quite a few points so please go through it once again for me at a much slower pace please as I am slow on the uptake."

Belle glared at him and repeated the whole thing again. He came over to the board and perused the drawings. "Is this your work too?"

Bertram jumped up and went to the board. "Miss Harcourt is our top artist and yes this is also her work, a very talented lady if I may say so."

"So I see, most impressive." Mark replied. He put his hand out to Belle and with a winsome smile added, "I think we can do business. I like your work very much and it is very twenty-first century, which is what I was looking for. Meet me for dinner tonight and we can go over a few points and maybe clinch the deal."

Belle refused his hand. "Sorry I am busy tonight." She replied just a bit too quickly making it perfectly obvious.

"Tomorrow night then."

"I am busy for the next few weeks."

Bertram was looking daggers at her but Belle did not care she had no intentions of going anywhere with a rat like Mark Dawson.

"Then that is a great pity we could have sealed the deal today and the contract would have been in your pocket this very evening. Still, I will give it some thought and maybe I might get back to you." Mark shook Bertram's hand and stormed out the room leaving them in no doubt he extremely angry.

"What the bloody hell are you playing at? You had him in the palm of your hand and the contract could have been in your pocket tonight. What do you think you are doing and you never said you were involved with Harcourt Services? I should have realised the connection."

"I did not know it was Harcourt's we were dealing with as you never said and I did not want to go out to dinner with him." Belle was collecting all her things.

"You take other clients out for dinner to conclude a deal, what is so different this time?"

"I don't like him"

"Like, what the bloody hell has like to do with anything. This is business and his business is gigantic and we need it badly. I tell you this if we lose this contract because of your outrageous behaviour today I will see to it you never work in advertising ever again."

Belle was not sure what to say. "Look he liked it so get someone else to snuggle up to him I don't mind stepping aside."

"He went out of here like a raging lion I hope for your sake he gets in touch if not you are out, understood?"

When Mark left the room he was irate. He had been surprised yet very pleased to see her again. He had understood Belinda Harcourt and he had buried the hatchet at the solicitor's office, it was clear she had not, so her apology had was worthless.

She had rushed through the presentation and it was obvious she wished to leave as quickly as possible. Did he smell or something? Well if they wanted his business he would make sure they toed his line and so would bloody Belinda Harcourt. What a coincidence though and he wondered why she had never worked for her Father she would have been a great asset. The presentation was brilliant; he knew he would get no better elsewhere.

He caught up with Bertram just as they were leaving. "A word please."

Belle hurried past. "I will wait in the car"

"I only work with the person involved and if Miss Harcourt is too busy to seal the deal with dinner then forget it I will look elsewhere. I want this advertising up and running so have no time to waste. What does Miss Harcourt imagine I am going to do, embarrass her in an exclusive restaurant or do I smell? She ran through the presentation as if she could not get away quickly enough."

"I am deeply sorry about that, I am sure she is just not at her best today, time of the month and all that and the ladies do get temperamental at these times."

"Complete garbage who do you think you are talking to. I will be at the Royal tomorrow evening eight sharp, if she does not attend you can say goodbye to any contract now or in the future, I bid you good day sir."

Mark walked away with a smile on his face. Bertram would see to it she attended and maybe they could start to get to know each other properly. There was something about her an allure that drew him to her and he wished to find out all about her. So what, he had used blackmail for the first time in his life but it was excusable under the circumstances.

There was no conversation on the drive back to the agency. Bertram was absolutely livid with Belle and her performance, she had rushed through the presentation as if she had a train to catch and she had been downright rude to Dawson as well, what the hell was she playing at? He did not want to lose Belle she was a great asset but he could not afford to lose the contract either. It needed some diplomacy on his part, he had to get her to agree this dinner engagement and nail that elusive contract. Maybe it was time to be honest and tell her the truth he had to do something to win this contract and save the agency.

Chapter 15

"Did we get the contract?" Bob enquired as soon as they appeared.

"It is pending." Bertram said brusquely. "Come into my office Belinda."

She knew when he called her that it was a very bad sign.

"Sit down Belinda, now are you going to tell me what you have against this man?"

"It is personal." Belle replied quietly.

"In business we leave personalities out of the equation. You have wined and dined numerous clients and this is no different. If you wish to succeed in business you put your personal feelings to one side. I am sure you have not liked every client you went to dinner with so I see no problem here. I will tell you honestly if we do not secure this contract with Mark Dawson the agency is finished. I have already made out the redundancy notices to all the staff but held back in the hope we would get this contract and save the business. I tell you this in strict confidence."

Belle knew she was in a tight corner and there was nothing she could do but agree to the dinner engagement. "I will go." She declared in a quiet voice.

"If you go you must treat him well, allow him to think you like him and admire him. Use your charms to get the contract signed. If this is impossible we will close the agency doors now. The last thing I want is a replay of today's fiasco, you ran through the campaign as if you were rushing to catch a bloody train and to make matters worse you were downright rude to the man. I tried to make excuses but the man is anything but stupid and you put me in a very difficult position with your behaviour."

"You will be asking me to sleep with him next."

"If that is what it takes to save this agency then yes." Bertram replied red in the face with anger. "Sorry that was unforgivable, of course I draw the line at you actually sleeping with him. I like to think I am an honourable man."

"I will charm the birds out of the trees just for you."

"Thank you, I will not forget who saved the agency. You can leave early and decide what to wear tomorrow evening. Take tomorrow off and have your hair done or what women usually do, anything to impress the man. You have the looks use them; just remember everything now depends on you. Oh!

And I do not want you sleeping with him, sorry about that remark."

Belle went home and she was not happy, she knew Bertram was correct this was only business but it did not help her to remember that. Of all the rotten luck, she had never thought for a second she was doing a presentation for her Father's business no, not her Father's but sneaky Dawson's business now.

She called Mark Dawson thinking this was the second time she had to humiliate herself with him and she hated it but informed him she was free tomorrow evening if the invitation was still open.

"Good, we can get to know each other and maybe seal the deal I will send a car for you."

"There is no need I will come in my own car just tell me where and when."

"We will have wine for dinner, you cannot drink and drive that would be very irresponsible. See you tomorrow evening." Mark hung up on her.

She stamped her foot, now she would have to wait until he saw fit to drive her home and she was not pleased.

CHAPTER 16

Belle dressed to kill the next evening; Mark Dawson had been seen with models and actresses so she intended to show him how she could dazzle if she chose and also to let him know she was not riff raff.

She wore a dark green velvet dress that was strapless and more or less backless which she had designed herself some time ago but had never worn. It seemed to mould to her figure and she was pleased at the effect when she looked in the mirror. A bit too much cleavage perhaps but if you have it flaunt it. She wore her hair up and fixed with a diamante clasp.

Sophisticated and very presentable she thought with a clear sign, look but do not touch. She sat down to wait for the car and began to doodle on an old envelope that was on the table then she remembered her mobile, must have that with me and she ran to fetch it just as the doorbell rang. She grabbed her purse put her phone in and rushed to the door.

"Car for Miss Harcourt." The chauffeur told her.

"Thank you." Belle closed the door and was escorted to the limousine. On the way she began to get very nervous, maybe she was overdressed for the Royal.

"How do you think I look, be honest now."

The chauffeur smiled, "I think you are much nicer than any model I have driven around, you look good enough to eat miss."

Belle relaxed and began to enjoy being driven in the huge car just like royalty.

Mark was waiting at the restaurant and escorted her to her seat. "You look breathtaking." He told her.

"Thank you, I do scrub up well." She bit her tongue, she was going to charm the man not kill him.

"Sorry, that was not meant how it sounded."

"If we are to do business I suggest we forget about our past difficulties and start afresh tonight."

"I don't remember any past difficulties." Belle gave him her charm the birds out of the trees smile.

"Good now we can enjoy each others company and get to know each other better."

Belle allowed him to order for her, yet another way to inflate his ego. He talked about himself during the meal and Belle learned quite a bit about him and she had to admit he was not the ruthless businessman she had first thought.

Their hands touched when they both lifted their wine glasses and the touch seemed to electrify her. He wanted to know all about her but Belle was not about to tell him her life story all she wanted from him was his signature on the silly contract.

"You are a brilliant artist." He told her over coffee.

"I love drawing, I used to draw caricatures for the university magazine got into hot water once when one of the professors realised it was him and did not take it kindly." Belle laughed.

"When you laugh it is like heavenly music."

When Belle looked at his face he seemed serious.

You must have kissed the blarney
stone." She replied her face glowing.

"I rather like you Belinda Harcourt."

"Call me Belle everyone else does."

"I like that, Belle means beautiful and
you are certainly that and more."

She felt her face flush yet again.

"Now this contract, you wish me to sign
it?"

"It does not have to be tonight." She did
not want to seem too eager. "Only if
you are pleased with the presentation of
course."

"I am very impressed with all your work
and yes the contract is yours. I think
you and I make a good team. Now if
you are ready we will go back to my
suite in the hotel and sign the papers."

She was speechless; going back to his
hotel room was not part of the plan. Did
he intend she sleep with him? If so he
was out of luck.

"Don't you have the papers with you?"

He smiled and she felt her resolve
fading fast.

"I am not in the habit of carrying papers to dinner dates."

"This is business not a date." Belle corrected him quickly.

"That is a great pity as I have enjoyed your company tonight and had hoped to repeat it."

She could think of nothing to say to that.

"I can assure you, you will be quite safe. I am a business man but also a gentleman. Mark stood up and led her to the limousine. She felt she had no choice but to do as he asked. She had worked hard all evening to charm him and she was determined to have the signed contract in her pocket this very night.

Once in his suite Mark poured her a nightcap. "We will drink a toast to a new and rewarding relationship." He produced the contract and Belle felt a glow when she watched him sign.

"Now your signature." Her handed her his gold pen and held on to her hand when she was taking it. "Belle you are a most beautiful lady and also very talented. You are wasted at the agency. Why not come and work for me. You will have so much more scope and also more money. I wonder why you did not work for your Father seems rather strange given your talent."

The mention of her Father made her blood boil. "I would never work for you and you know why." She pulled her

hand away and quickly signed the contract.

She was shaking when she put the contract in her bag and dropped her bag with all the contents falling out on to the carpet. They banged their heads together when they both went down on their knees to retrieve the items.

Mark put his arms round her and kissed her full on the lips. "I have longed to do that all evening."

She felt as if everything was going round and round and before she could stop herself she began to respond to his kiss. She managed to pull herself away when she remembered who and what he was. "I must go it is rather late I will call for a taxi."

"No need Charles my chauffeur will take you home."

"I would rather take a taxi thank you."

"Don't be downright ridiculous. You have the contract that is why you have been so charming tonight. Do not take me for a fool Belle; you have what you came for. None the less I did enjoy your company tonight and intend we see a great deal of each other in the future."

"No you will not, I will see to that."

"You are my advertising agent are you not? You have just signed to say you are."

Belle stared at him. "You would not dare."

"Yes indeed I would, I intend to check every little detail of the campaign and to do that I require to see you in person."

"You are a heel and an unscrupulous lout."

"So are you Miss Harcourt using your charms in such a fashion this evening yes, a real temptress and you deserve an Oscar. As I said earlier we make a good team. I must warn you before you go not to wear that dress again as it sends my heart racing. You would have been more covered in a bathing suit as the dress leaves little to the imagination. Very tempting indeed, just as well I am a true gentleman after your sexy performance this evening." Mark laughed.

"I loathe you and all you stand for. You think you have won the war but you have only won two little skirmishes. I intend to put you in your place and win the final battle. I hate you and everything you stand for. Now you can go run to your bloody solicitor but this time it is my word against yours." Belle grabbed her bag and made for the door.

"What about a goodnight kiss to seal our deal?"

"Go to hell." Belle replied as she banged the door shut.

Mark picked up the envelope on the carpet after she left and looked at it. He laughed at what he saw, a caricature of himself and he had to admit it was good very good indeed. He intended to have it framed and put up on his office wall. Who knows it might even be worth a lot of money one day. He wished now he had not kissed her as it had captured his heart and he knew there was only one woman for him now and that was Belle Harcourt, he was now totally enmeshed in her web and he was actually elated.

Chapter 17

Once Belle was home safe and sound she breathed a sigh of relief, she had been very tempted to see what enfolded after that kiss. It had felt strange yet very pleasant indeed. She had never been in love and wondered if it was anything like the sensation of kissing Mark Dawson.

Forget about him she told herself, I have the contract so I have won this battle and come out unscathed. Bertram will be really pleased with me; I have saved the agency and have earned a huge bonus as well. A very good night's work. She stared in the mirror, there was nothing wrong with the dress it was just his dirty mind at work again. That was another trait he had that disgusted her.

Next morning when Belle entered the office everyone applauded.

"News travels fast." She grinned.

"Bertram is waiting in the office for you and he is all smiles for a change. Congratulations Belle." Bob shook her hand.

"Come in Belle, you have surpassed yourself this time and we have Mark Dawson tied up to us for four whole years. We are on the top this time and we have you to thank. We are now one of the top agencies in London and once the news gets around everyone will want to come to us."

"It was not as bad as expected, the man can be charming when he wants to be."

"Glad to hear that as he requests your attendance in his suite at two today. Points that have to be ironed out so he says."

"Find someone else I have done what you wanted, now I don't wish to be in his company ever again."

"I am afraid that is not possible, Dawson added a paragraph to the original contract that the only contact with the agency must be with Belinda Harcourt. The contract is forfeited if this is not adhered to."

"Why the sneaky rat, did you know about this?"

"No I did not, Dawson had it added when you refused to go to dinner with him. You must have dented his pride somewhat."

"This means I am at his beck and call for four years."

"I am afraid so." Bertram replied with a frown. "What on earth have you against this man? He does a lot of good work and he is one of the few honest businessmen around."

"As I said it is personal, I suppose now it is signed I have no option but to do as he pleases. I will however forget all about charming the client. If we are tied to him for four lousy years he is also tied to me for four years. I will make his life utterly miserable I promise you."

"For god's sake you cannot do that you are in the wrong here not him with your belligerent attitude. He can take us to court and with his money he would win and what happens to the agency then. Do you want us all to be on the breadline just to gratify some absurd inane whim you have."

"Actually it is anything but a whim but a matter of loyalty."

"Your loyalty lies with this agency now don't you think?"

She had to agree with him but it did not stop her being upset. Four years was a very long time to be polite to Mark Dawson her sworn enemy.

"I promise I will be on my best behaviour, I will treat him like my other clients he will have no complaints in this direction I promise you."

"Thank you, I can begin to breath again. I just wish I knew what history you have with this man that makes you so determined to loathe him, he is well respected everywhere else and is very generous to his chosen charities. I would not be surprised if he ends up with a knighthood."

"Well here is one that does not respect him and never will but I will behave in a business like manner. I am going back home to get changed for this so called meeting."

"You are fine as you are." Bertram replied.

"Much too severe." Belle replied as she walked out.

She was not a happy bunny, she wondered what would happen if she no longer worked at the agency. Dawson could hardly go to court if that happened. No, on second thoughts that was a very bad idea. She had a big house but so was the upkeep and she needed the money, damn and blast the man he had her cornered and there was nothing she could do about it but bide her time until she acquired the shares she required to see him squirm and she could hardly wait for that special day to dawn. "I will vindicate you Father just be patient a little longer." She said to his photograph.

Chapter 18

Belle turned up for the meeting wearing very tight jeans and a t-shirt with untouchable blazoned across the front and her hair in a ponytail. The secretary gave her a look of disapproval as she sent her in.

"Good afternoon Belle." Mark held his hand out and she shook it but was bitterly disappointed, as he did not seem to notice how she was dressed he was supposed to be affronted.

"Good afternoon Mr Dawson can we get down to business as I have another appointment with a client in an hour."

Mark grinned. "Do you know your face gives you away each time you tell a lie?"

Belle chose to ignore the remark and hoped the meeting would be short but it seemed he had many points to iron out and finally she lost concentration and became distracted.

She shifted in her seat a few times, crossed and uncrossed her legs, she was very uncomfortable and he kept droning on about this and that and she was not really listening. She could not take her eyes off his lips when he talked

and she kept remembering the feeling
when their lips had touched it had been
sheer magic, she wouldn't mind a replay
and there was his dimple, really cute. If
he had not been her sworn enemy she
would have leapt over the desk and
mauled him.

"You agree then, that indeed is splendid
thank you very much I do appreciate it."

Belle gave herself a mental shake what
had he been saying and more to the
point what had she just agreed to. She
could hardly ask him to repeat it; she
just prayed it wasn't anything
important.

Mark was in his element; she had
clearly not been paying attention and
had been in a world of her own for some
time now. He had taken advantage,
shame on him. The way she was
dressed was supposed to tell him
something but it only emphasised that
she would look good in anything, even a
paper sack.

This woman was something else, he had
been attracted to her from the first time
he had set eyes on her but she had
taken against him for reasons he could
not understand. He had taken the
opportunity to kiss her and it had been

fatal for him. He now wanted to know all about her, what made her tick, he had seen a glimpse of her stunning body and he wanted all of her, her heart and her soul. He wanted it so much it was beginning to take over his life as he could think of nothing else these days and is was becoming a real addiction.

Mark made up reasons to check out points of the campaign just to keep her close to him for a short while longer. When he ran out of points to consider Belle was quickly on her feet.

"If that is all I really must be going, I have a mountain of paperwork to deal with back at the agency."

"Then I will not keep you any longer, until tonight." Mark attempted to take her hand but she turned away.

"Tonight! What arrangements for tonight?" Belle had a blank look on her face.

"As I said before Charles will pick you up at eight. The Ball is a charity event a very lavish dressy affair."

"Are you sure I agreed to this, I don't remember anything about a ball being mentioned? I don't have anything to wear at so short notice."

"The green evening gown will be splendid whoever designed it clearly had you in mind."

"It is my own design actually. Oh! Well I did agree so be it I never go back on my word."

When she took her leave Mark laughed out loud, then he felt really guilty. He had been underhand and duped her into attending the ball with him naughty boy that he was but he was thrilled nevertheless to share another evening with her, maybe this time they would end friends which would be an excellent start.

Belle on the other hand was trying to remember if he had mentioned any ball and decided she would need to be on her mettle every time she was with him. Daydreaming about a kiss was obviously fatal; she prayed that was all she had agreed to.

Mark was in the car when she was picked up. He took her breath away in his dinner suit; he looked marvellous and so very handsome. It would do her no harm to be seen on the arm of this hunk she thought to herself.

"It will be a late affair so I have booked you a room at the hotel for tonight."

"You should have warned me." Belle
said testily.

"You clearly have forgotten, I did inform
you of all the arrangements at our
afternoon meeting. He gave her a
dazzling smile and she wished he would
not smile at her like that, any resolve
she might have just seemed to melt.

"I have left all you may require for an
overnight stay in the room for you and
clothes for the morning as it seems you
have a bad memory. I suggest you get
into the habit of taking notes to help
you as you did not remember the ball
either."

"Thank you sir for your observation I
will keep that in mind." Belle retorted.
She still could not remember him
speaking about any ball earlier in the
day but he must have done; yet there
was nothing wrong with her memory,
which happened to be very good
normally.

CHAPTER 19

When they arrived Mark was treated like royalty and as his partner she received the same treatment. She found out later Mark had organised the ball to collect donations for a hospital project he wished to build in Africa.

She felt like a fish out of water at first among all these powerful and wealthy people. Mark seemed to know how she was feeling and never left her side. They danced and she felt she was in paradise when he held her in his arms and wanted to dance with him all night long, she was in heaven and wanted to stay there for as long as possible.

Mark as the organiser was expected to make a speech and he took Belle up to the dais with him.

"I don't belong here." She whispered.

"You are just as good in fact better than any person here and that includes me. I want you by my side."

"Is this part of the contract?"

"No, but it is what I wish. I want everyone here to know you are with me."

"But you are used to high class models and the like." Belle replied.

"No model can hold a candle to you my sweet Belinda."

She did not know why but she longed to kiss him right there and then.

Mark said his piece and spoke about the hospital in Africa in great detail and how many lives depended on it "I am donating half a million to this project and I hope all here will be just as generous."

Belle got carried away with his eloquent speech and could not resist it; she stood up and kissed him on the cheek and every one applauded.

"Thank you I am sure the money will roll in after your affectation."

Belle felt as if she had been slapped. "It was meant as an honest gesture, I'm sorry if I have embarrassed you I just got carried away with your fantastic speech."

Mark took her up to dance and held her very close. "I am very sorry I misconstrued your show of affection."

He danced to the middle of the floor and kissed her on the lips for all to see. She felt her knees go weak and she was sure she felt his tongue as he kissed her.

"I am tired, I really need to sit down"

"So you felt it too, I think I am falling in love with you sweet Belinda."

After they sat down Belle was inundated with requests to dance and felt she could not refuse any one of them and people donating to his hospital had surrounded Mark.

When the last dance was announced Mark made sure she danced with him. He held her close but said nothing; he was enjoying just holding her close in his arms and wished it would never end, he was besotted with her now and was well and truly trapped in her web and he was ecstatic.

Belle's feelings for him had changed and she did not understand why. He was still the man that had taken everything away from her Father and left him a broken man. She felt she was betraying her Father by even being in Mark's company, as for liking him she wondered who the real traitor was now and where had her loyalty suddenly disappeared to.

Mark escorted her to her room in the hotel, which turned out to be a suite.

"A room was all I required."

"Nothing but the best for my sweet
Belinda thank you for a most enjoyable
evening." He kissed her goodnight and
left.

Mark had thought of everything she
would need. Toothbrush, nightdress,
clothes for the morning and surprisingly
they looked as if they were the correct
size, even down to face-wipes to
remove her make-up.

She lay in bed and wondered what it
would be like to share his bed and give
herself to him. She had enjoyed a
glorious evening; it would have been
the icing on the cake if she had been in
his bed and enjoyed a glorious night.
She fell asleep only to dream of being in
his arms making exquisite love then felt
like a real Judas.

Chapter 20

Mark knocked on her door at nine the next morning. "Hope I am not too early."

"Come in I am just about ready to leave."

"I have ordered breakfast for us, thought we could eat together."

"I can eat breakfast at home."

"Too late it is on its way up." Mark smiled "I have received donations for the hospital in excess of one million, I think it is because of you. Didn't I say we made a good team? This hospital means a great deal to me and now it will be built and fitted out with the very best of equipment and save a great many lives and I want to thank you."

Belle was astounded. "A million that is absolutely amazing and simply terrific. It had nothing to do with me though you are a very generous man and that speech you made must have stirred up many peoples compassion."

"I do as much as possible for charities, I am from a humble background, but last evening was completely different. For once I had a partner by my side that made the evening so much more rewarding. I loathe attending such functions on my own, I do hope we can do it again."

"You don't need me." Belle said looking at him to see if he was really serious.

"Belle I have been successful in business and like to think honest. I am however alone and extremely lonely. I live in a hotel not a home and have no one to share anything with. I have always believed the right person would come along one day and make my life complete. I had begun to think this would never happen as I have waited a very long time. Then suddenly you Belle came into my life and changed everything. You think I destroyed your Father, I can honestly say that is not the case. I wish you to see all the papers and then you will believe me and maybe even begin to like me."

Everything was going really well until Mark mentioned her Father. She had been listening to his every word and believing his every word until he brought her Father into it. She remembered how he looked the last time she saw him, a sad broken man. She was betraying her own flesh and blood in the worst possible way and it had to stop now.

She picked up her evening gown and purse then without saying a single word she left the room. She heard him call out her name but she ignored it. Last evening had been a fantasy and she was happy she had finally come back down to earth. She was determined to see he got what was coming to him one way or another for her Father's demise. It was as if Mark Dawson had put a gun to her Father's head.

When she went to pay at reception she became even angrier. Dawson owned the hotel and there was no bill to pay and she wanted nothing from him.

Mark was left completely devastated, he had more or less told her he loved her but she had thrown it back in his face as if it were something vile. He knew he could have any woman he wanted but it was a huge joke as he only wanted his sweet Belinda and she was out of his reach all because of a silly small business that had been going down the drain. Any joy he had at the ball had just been completely destroyed, even the money he had collected for his pet project meant nothing to him now.

He knew now he faced a bleak future, no need to wait for the right woman to come along she had been and was now quickly gone and he did not think he could spend his whole life alone and without love.

Chapter 21

Belle called in sick something she would never have contemplated doing before, she was afraid Mark would demand to see her and she could not face him. She now knew he really was an honourable man but his connections with her Father made it impossible to associate with him other than business. It appalled her as she knew she had real feelings for him. "What do I do now Dad?" She asked his photograph, but he just stared back at her.

To vent her feelings she wrote a letter to Mark, one he would never read.

My Darling Mark,

You are the love of my life and I do not know how I can continue to live without you, as you are the very air that I breathe. I lie here in bed and imagine what it would be like to have you here beside me and it brings me great pain and copious tears, but my hands are tied by circumstances and loyalty to my Father and I could not live with myself if I turned traitor. You kissed me at the ball and I wanted to be with you and belong to you so much I was weak at the knees and in the hotel suite I desperately wanted you beside me. Why did I fall in love with you? Life can be so cruel, I have lost my Father and I cannot have you, my heart is breaking and I do not know how or why I should carry on. I dearly wish you find happiness elsewhere but wish it could have been with me and whomever you later marry I bloody hate her.

Bitter Belinda.

Belle folded the letter put it in an envelope then stuck it into a file out of sight out of mind. She had opened her heart now she had to forget him and learn to live without him or his love and she knew it would be anything but pleasant but she had no other option.

The papers had made a big splash over the ball and they had photographs of her and Mark so she cut them out and put them in a drawer. There was the one where Mark was kissing her and they both looked totally absorbed in each other. She put that one on her bedside table so she could remember every little detail and dream of what might have been.

Mark decided to be honest; in any case he could not face Belle knowing she would never be his. He called the agency only to be told Belle was not there. He spoke to Bertram and said he wished someone other than Belle to handle his advertising account. Bertram asked what was wrong. "Nothing is wrong, everything is simply perfect but on second thoughts I would prefer a man to liase with this time, no disrespect to Miss Harcourt intended I hasten to add. Her campaign is faultless very ingenious, exactly what I was looking for."

When Belle went back to work the next day and Bob informed her they were sharing the bonus and why, she was angry at Mark and yet pleased she would have no further contact with him. All he need do was smile at her and she was willing to surrender. Now she would never be tempted again to forget where her loyalties really lay.

She sent him e-mail and stated it had been nice doing business with him but he was old-fashioned in the extreme in regarding women in business as inferior to the male. I am just as good if not better than any male and that includes you a real chauvinist pig I may say. However you have done me a favour, as I am pleased we will have no further contact as my loyalties lie with my Father whom you dispatched so readily and quickly. I am sure the advertising campaign will go really well as it was I who designed it a mere puny female only fit for the kitchen sink and making babies. She signed it Emancipated Belinda.

When Mark read the e-mail he smiled, she would have made an exceptional wife for him and the thought of making babies with her was just about too much for him to bear. But he had to face the facts no matter what he did he could never please her and the thought of never seeing her again broke his heart. Everything he had worked for now seemed to turn to dust and all over a stupid little company that was failing and he had to go and fall in love with the daughter who did not know the true facts and was extremely loyal to her Father which in a way he admired.

The weeks went by and Belle tried very hard to rid Mark Dawson from her personal life and she was finding it nigh on impossible. She would lie in bed and wonder what it would be like to have him right here beside her. To have his lips on her mouth again and his arms holding her in close. It was futile and soul-destroying, she called him all the beastly names she could think of but it did not stop her from missing him and feeling very unhappy, but her loyalty to her Father forbade any personal contact with the man.

"I am miserable Father and whatever I do I cannot win." The photograph just smiled back at her.

CHAPTER 22

A shareholders meeting was notified for the following week and Belle intended to go and disrupt everything and anything she could, she owed it to her Father. She would speak to other shareholders and try to buy them out even if she had to mortgage the house; she wanted to see justice done and her Father could then rest in peace.

Belle decided to power dress for the meeting and turned up looking invincible, or so she hoped. She spoke to six shareholders before the meeting trying to convince them to sell. Three had already promised the shares to Mark and even when she upped the price they refused. Two who now knew the company was in the black decided to keep their shares. One she was actually successful with but it was not what she wanted as Mark had also increased his shares and she was still trailing well behind.

During the meeting when Mark put the accounts before them and asked for acceptance. Belle without taking in any details stood up and asked as many questions as she could think of but eventually the accounts were seconded. When he put forward his future plans for the company Belle again stood up and challenged each and every one of them just for the sake of it but eventually they too were accepted. She knew she was on a loser even before she left home but anything to thwart Mark was admissible to her. He had got everything through but he had to fight for each single one and that made her feel she was standing up for her Father.

She expected Mark to speak to her after the meeting closed but he just lifted all his papers and left the room without even looking in her direction and it nearly finished her. What was all this backbiting about she wondered and where was it getting her? Certainly not happiness, the opposite if she was being truthful. "What do I do now Dad?" She cried out in pain.

Mark had been happy to catch sight of Belle again but he told himself she was beyond reach and he should forget her, which was not an easy task. He lay in bed at night and thought about her all the time and how exquisite it had been to kiss her. He determined he could not go through the rest of his life alone living in hotel rooms. He desperately wanted a home and someone to share his life with; he could not have Belle so he would need to settle for second best. He began to look around for a suitable partner again.

Mark dated a few women and finally chose Ellen a top model. She was nothing compared to his sweet Belinda but he felt he could no longer tolerate being on his own. Life was for living not just existing from one day to the next. If he put his mind to it he could pretend to be happy and at least he would no longer be on his own and that had to be good. After a very short romance the papers announced their engagement and when Belle read it she was heart-broken.

He was a bounder, telling her he loved her then two minutes later marrying some upstart of a model. She had had a lucky escape she tried hard to tell herself, but she was still devastated by the news.

Belle lifted the box with all her Father's papers and finally began to go through them. As she progressed she was utterly dismayed, her Father's business had been in a very precarious place and he had even started to think about mortgaging the house to keep the business afloat. If Mark had not come along she would not have had a roof over her head. It all came down to one simple fact; her Father had not been the businessman she had thought or at least he had lost his touch when her Mother died. She could see mismanagement all along the line; it was surprising he had lasted as long as he did. He had been stressed out for many months, that was what caused his heart attack not losing his company to Mark Dawson. The one thing that stuck in Belle's throat was how her Father had lied to her for all that time. Now she knew why he had said she would never work in the company and why he had said sorry just before he died. "What have you done Dad? You have ruined my life that is what you have done."

Mark had made a hostile bid but he had wanted to keep her Father in the business and also the name Harcourt Services. Further on she found out it was Uncle Giles who approached Mark, not the other way round as she had been informed. No wonder Uncle Giles had sold out, like a rat deserting a sinking ship. How could she have been so blind, no wonder her Father had refused to allow her to work with him but if he had they might have been able to save the company that meant so much to him.

She cringed when she remembered all the vile names she had called Mark, it was unforgivable and she had never given him the opportunity of a rebuttal. She had thrown her future happiness away with her misplaced loyalty and also given pain to the one person who was innocent in all of this Mark Dawson.

Belle fretted endlessly over how she had wronged Mark and wanted to put it right. If only she had taken the time to look through her Father's papers immediately. It was even possible Mark could have loved her; he had more or less had told her this after that marvellous ball. She knew she had thrown away something so precious that life would never be the same again. Love like that only happened once in a lifetime and she had discarded it like it was rubbish and wounded Mark at the same time and she deserved all the misery heaped upon her.

It was important to her that Mark was informed that she now knew the truth and she wished to make recompense, but how? The shares of course, she would sell him the shares and then he would understand how sorry she really was.

Belle wrote to Belton his solicitor explaining how she had wronged Mark and apologising profusely for her error in judgment and offering her shares to Mark at their market price. She ended by wishing him a very long and happy marriage. The last part nearly tore her heart out; as she knew it could have been her he was marrying if she had not been so foul mouthed and utterly stupid.

She turned her Father's photograph face down, as she was very angry he had lied to her.

Mark was devastated when he read her letter. He had given up hope he could ever have her as his partner and now he was committed to Ellen who was a mediocre second best to sweet Belinda.

He was a gentleman so the marriage would go ahead as he had made a commitment. It broke his heart in two when he thought if he had been more patient Belle could have been his. Well the dye was cast and that was the end, he would marry next month as arranged and spend the rest of his life with a woman he did not love and pretend to be happy. "Serves me bloody well right." He told the caricature on the wall.

Mark never replied to Belle's letter. He did not want the shares he wanted her and that was impossible now and he would have to learn to live with the pretence that he was happy and it was going to be very difficult indeed.

When Mark met Ellen that same evening he felt sick at the act he had to put on and it was not fair on Ellen. She put her arms round him and tried to kiss him and he turned his face away. He was well aware that yet again she was pestering him to sleep with her but he refused as always, the very idea repulsed him and yet she was a real beauty but she was not his sweet Belinda and never would be.

"What is wrong with me? Since the day we met you have avoided spending the night with me. You never touch me or kiss me, am I so bloody awful?"

"You are a beautiful lady but I am a gentleman, I wish to wait until we are married and do things properly."

"In this day and age who the hell acts like that, there is something wrong about all this and I know it is not me. I can have any man I wish and by bad luck I chose you. You make me feel ugly and undesirable with no sex appeal. There is something wrong with you I know there is, no wonder you have never been married you are a right cold fish if you ask me. You are not homosexual are you? That wouldn't surprise me in the least. I don't want children as I have my figure to consider but I could never live without a good sex life and I know I can never have that if I married you. This has been a quick engagement but it will be very short, I no longer wish to marry you. I will keep the ring for the entire trauma you have put me through and good riddance." Ellen flounced out her head held high.

Mark did not even call her back; he was so relieved she had finished with him. He had not wanted to hurt her she was the innocent in all this but actually making love to her had been abhorrent to him. There was only one person in this whole world who could satisfy his desires sexual or otherwise and that was Belle Harcourt. He felt as if a huge load had been taken off his shoulders now that Ellen had set him free, but he felt a heel at the way he had treated Ellen.

He wanted to see Belle immediately and propose again but rejected the idea. Maybe she did not love him, he had nearly married someone he did not love and that had been a dreadful thing to do, Ellen had had a lucky escape. What if Belle married him out of guilt not love, he could not even bear the thought. Yet, when he had kissed her he felt that spark between them and he was sure it was not wishful thinking. He had been alone for a long long time another few weeks would not kill him so he decided to wait. Be patient everything comes to him who waits and he consoled himself

with that thought, but underneath the
surface he felt the excitement bubbling
up, sweet Belinda might be his after all.

Chapter 23

Belle hated herself and was miserable most of the time. She looked around and saw nothing to be cheerful about, everything looked the same dull and uninviting, even the weather was against her and she could not lift her sprits no matter how hard she tried. "What a miserable lonely and horrible life I have made for myself."

Finally trying to boost herself into doing something positive she resigned from the agency it had only been a means to an end; nothing seemed to satisfy her these days.

Bertram was not happy at her decision. "We have made our name and many of the top companies are coming to us so I really need you to stay. I know by your demeanour you are not happy about something is it because you only received half the bonus on that Dawson deal you certainly came up with a superb campaign but I thought it was only fair to split it between you and Bob as he will be the liaison man?"

"I was happy to split the bonus and as you say it was fair. Money is not the issue but I feel I have to move on for personal reasons that I would rather not discuss."

"Well I will not press you on the subject but I will be sorry to lose you and if you ever wish to come back there will always be a place here for you."

"Thank you Bertram if it is okay I will leave at the end of the week and I would rather you told the rest of the staff after I have left."

"As you wish, I also wish you every success in your next venture but doubt if you need it as you are a very talented lady."

Belle left the agency on the Friday.

"See you on Monday." They chorused not realising they would never see her again. It was the way she wanted it, as she hated farewell parties.

CHAPTER 24

Belle roamed around the length and breadth of the country photographing anything that drew her eye and she set up a darkroom in the house to develop all her own work. She even attempted painting again but her heart was not in it. To earn some money for the upkeep of the house she designed some clothes for a fashion house, which kept the wolf from the door. She still had her Father's photograph face down, as she was still very angry at his deceit.

She even spent a few days in Italy and tried very hard to enjoy taking snaps of all the ancient buildings to be had there but she got no joy from it so returned home very quickly. The house was empty and so was she, could she live the rest of her life alone and unloved until the day she died she often wondered? What an appalling prospect, she would never know what love was and she admitted it was her own fault entirely, her misguided loyalty to her Father had made sure of that.

Often she would look at the newspaper cutting of Mark kissing her and it always brought tears to her eyes. The thought he was making love to the model he married made her cringe. She hoped he was happy he certainly deserved to be and he now had his beautiful wife to accompany him to all future balls, he was no longer alone or lonely and she was happy for him but nonetheless she hated this wife of his whoever she was.

"It could have been me, it should have been me." She cried out in torment. Each day that passed the pain seemed to deepen that little bit more and it was becoming almost unbearable.

Finally one day Belle looked around her and decided enough was enough she could take no more anguish and decided to make a new life for herself abroad, well away from anything to do with Mark Dawson. He was always in the papers for something or other and she wanted no more of it. She put the house up for sale determined to go ahead with her plans. One way or another she had to get him out of her system and face life without him. In any case she did not deserve him she had gone in guns blazing without even checking her facts and had been foul-mouthed into the bargain she was certainly no lady and unfit company for someone such as Mark Dawson.

Mark's estate agent gave him a call." I think we have found the perfect house for you sir."

"Good, I am sick to death living in hotel rooms. Where is it?"

"Barnet Road number two"

Mark was surprised at Belle selling the house, he thought she would never do that it was a beautiful house. He hoped she was not in financial trouble.

"Put in an offer full asking price with twenty percent on top. No mention of my name, understood?"

"Leave it to me sir, don't you wish to view it first?"

"I know the house and I must have it, if you have to up the price you have my permission to do so, just make sure the house is mine whatever the cost. Remember I want my name kept out if it."

Mark was pleased when he was informed the house was now his, Belle would not be short of money now and when the time was right he would approach her and hope she would accept his proposal of marriage and they would live in the house together, sheer utter bliss. Just be patient a little bit longer he consoled himself and you will have the life you always yearned, this time with the right person.

The furniture Belle could not bear to part with was put in storage along with some personal belongings. She locked the door for the last time and felt saddened it had come to this but she could no longer bear to live in the house alone. It was a house built for a family with children running about, something she would never have. She hoped the new owner would love and care for it just as she had. She stood in the driveway took a long lingering last look, turned her back and walked away to a new life without Mark Dawson and also a home.

CHAPTER 25

Mark had a meeting with Bob from the agency about the advertising campaign and was distraught when he found out Belle no longer worked there and no one knew where she had gone.

"I think she went abroad but where to we do not know. She left us without a word so we could not wish her bon voyage. She was brilliant though don't you think? She was wasting her talents with us, I rather liked her she was a lovely person both inside and out."

"Yes indeed." Mark ended the meeting most abruptly as he choked on the words, it looked as if he had lost her forever this time and he should have approached her much earlier. Now his life was in ruins unless he could find her. As soon as he got rid of Bob he began to look for her.

Belle went to Norway why there she could not say it was as good a place as any the way she felt. With some of the money from the house sale she opened up her own photography business and spent every hour building up the business and began to be rather successful. She became well known in Norway and her work was much sought after, as for money it was rolling in and her bank balance had never looked so healthy. She was at a stage where she could pick and choose what work to accept which pleased her greatly but she was not concerned about the money, it was of no importance it was only a means to an end. As for happiness that had passed her by a long time ago or to be honest with herself she had thrown it away and she knew she deserved every miserable day of it.

Belle got tired so rather than work all hours of the day and night she began to accept dates, maybe she would find someone to marry and have a family. It would be second best but she could put up with that if she had children.

She met Carl at an exhibition and she quite liked him. He was pleasant and a good man, not as handsome as Mark but handsome enough and very attentive. He was rich so was not after her money, all in all he would do she thought and she could have children that would make up for having to settle for second best she decided.

Everything was going well and she had checked that Carl liked children. They liked the same things and enjoyed each others company and Belle felt he would definitely fill the huge gap in her life and she had chosen really well.

Then came his first passionate kiss and his intimate touch, this finished Belle completely. She had not liked the kiss at all, it felt decidedly wrong and she did not think it the least bit pleasant, his touch seemed out of place too and decidedly unpalatable. She could not imagine making love with him it made her cringe at the thought and even seemed dirty.

She could not understand why at first, then she realised she had tasted the best and knew without doubt second best would never satisfy her not in a million years and she balked at the very idea of having sex with Carl or anyone else except Mark Dawson. Now he was different altogether he was a real man, she was positive he would make love in the most exquisite manner, pity he was out of bounds these days.

Carl had been very irate with her when she dumped him and at first could not understand the reason why.

"We were good together, I was about to ask you to marry me then suddenly for no reason at all you rebuff me. I think there is something not quite right about you maybe you are doing me a huge favour."

"I am truly sorry and believe me I am doing you a favour. You see I am in love with someone else but it could never be

and I thought I could live with second
best that it would be sufficient if we had
children, but now I know it would never
work and it would be most unfair on
you."

"Second best indeed, thank you very
much for nothing. You know I
understood you to be a lovely lady
clearly I made a grave mistake, leading
me up the proverbial garden path and
then slamming the door on my face I
think you are a real two-timing bitch."
Carl marched off in a real angry mood.

Belle was really upset over Carl. She
had treated him shamefully but at least
she had not married him then found out
she could not live with him, at least she
had spared him that agony.

After parting company with Carl she was
very homesick and weary of Norway so
after a three-year stay she sold up and
moved back to London quite a rich
woman. She rented a flat hoping in time
she could buy back her old house and
stay there until her days were ended
She had come the full circle it seemed
and she was still very unhappy.

Her life from now on would be childless
and more importantly unloved and she
had brought it on herself with misguided
loyalty to her Father and for the first

time she felt sorry for him. So what he had lied to her and left her in this dismal miserable life but some of it was her own fault.

She had alienated Uncle Giles with her foul mouth and had no other family so she was truly alone in this horrible life.

" I forgive you Dad I know you loved me but who the hell is ever going to forgive me?" She turned the photograph the right way up and put it in a prominent place again.

Chapter 26

Belle had been back for three weeks before she went to view her old home and hoped to see children running about in the garden she had lovingly tended. When she arrived at the house what she saw shocked her to the core. Whoever had bought the house had allowed it to go to wreck and ruin. She peered in the filthy window and realised it was exactly how she had left it and she was furious. A beautiful Edwardian house left to rot and whoever owned it should be hung drawn and quartered and she would tell them so the very first chance she got. She was now determined more than ever to buy the house back before it fell down altogether and it would cost her a fortune in repairs to bring it back to its former glory.

The estate agent refused to give her any information. "The data protection act totally forbids it" She was informed. "We will however inform our client if you give us your details."

Belle left her phone number.

"We have a prospective buyer for the house in Barnet Road and they seem very keen to purchase sir."

"The house is not for sale." Mark said his voice quite angry at the very idea of selling the house.

When Belle received the message she was really angry. Why hold on to a house you did not want and worse still allow it to fall into total disrepair. She would not be put off and starting digging to find out the owner. She was very surprised when she found out Mark Dawson was said owner, what on earth was he thinking of? Probably that horrible model he had married thought the house was not grand enough for her, well she would not allow them to get away with wrecking a beautiful old house like this.

Belle phoned Mark's office and asked to speak to him.

"What is it about?"

"I wish to purchase number two Barnet Road."

"Hold the line please"

"There is a woman on the line she wants to buy the house in Barnet road sir."

"Inform her it is not for sale." Mark replied brusquely.

"I am sorry but the house is not for sale."
Belle erupted and insisted on speaking to Mr Dawson himself and before she could say another word she heard Mark's voice roaring down the line. "You

are the second person to enquire about this house. I will tell you the same as I told her, the house is not for sale now and never will be as long as I live so you are wasting your time and mine. Good day to you." Mark slammed the phone down on her.

"Why of all the bloody nerve." Belle fumed all day after that encounter and was determined to tell him what she thought of him.

She typed him a letter marking it personal and proceeded to tell him he should be ashamed of himself allowing a beautiful Edwardian house to slip into disrepair, you don't even have the excuse of not having the money for the upkeep. You and your wife should be living in the house and filling it with children but no doubt the house is not grand enough for her. You are a philistine and people such as you should not be allowed to own such a unique property. If you have no intention of living in it you should have the decency to sell it to someone who will care for it properly. If I had my way I would slap you in the mouth you objectionable ignorant little man.

Belle posted the letter and felt slightly better after venting her anger.

When Mark received the letter he actually smiled for the first time in years. The letter put him in mind of his sweet Belinda who had disappeared very soon after selling the house. He had tried to locate her to no avail.

The caustic remarks were exactly the sort Belle would have used. She did not mince her words whoever she was. He tore it up as it brought back too many painful memories of what he had lost. He could never live in that house nor could he ever sell it. The house could only accommodate two people, Belle and he so let it rot, he certainly did not care and the quicker it fell down the better he would feel.

Belle called Mark's office several times after that about selling the house hoping he would relent until eventually Mark gave orders to hang up on her when she called. The woman was turning out to be a real nuisance stirring up memories and desires he wished to forget and she refused to take no for an answer. He hated being rude but had no choice, let her pester someone else.

Belle just became more and more angry so she vented her anger with another epistle informing him he was allowing a lovely family home to go to waste and all because of a wife who obviously did not want children. I warn you now you will live to regret it you and that snobbish partner of yours. You are filthy rich in money but you have no social graces worth speaking about either of you, in fact you are both ignorant peasants and don't you dare hang up on me again you bloody barbarian.

When Mark read the letter he stared at it, if he did not know better he would have sworn it came from Belle but of course that was impossible she had made a life for herself abroad somewhere and forgotten all about him probably even married with a family by now. He hoped she was not happy she did not deserve happiness leaving him in this miserable lonely life. He wished he could have done the same; he had tried but failed miserably and each and every day was utterly wretched.

Chapter 27

Belle was out and about with her camera again when she spotted this little boy sitting on the pavement outside the main railway station. He looked a real waif with his dirty face and that lost hungry look with a plastic bag sitting by his side. Belle took his photograph and prepared to move on but he tugged at her heartstrings. She felt sorry for him as he could only be seven or eight years old, he looked alone which did not seem right especially outside a main train station, it could be a very dangerous place for any child on their own. Without thinking Belle turned back and approached him.

"Where is your Mother?"

"Don't have a Mum." He replied.

"Are you on your own?"

"Yip."

"Why are you sitting here all on your own are you waiting for someone?"

"Nope."

"Are you hungry?"

"Starvin no had me breakfast."

"If you wish you can come home with me and I will give you breakfast."

The boy quickly stood up and took Belle's hand.

"My name is Belle you will be safe with me, what is your name?"

"Sandy, I'm hungry can we go now?"

Belle hand in hand with Sandy walked back to her flat. She had a warm feeling with his hand in hers he was so trusting she wanted to cry. She made him a huge breakfast, which he bolted down; he clearly had not eaten for some time.

"Where do you live Sandy?"

"Got no place I ave run away again."

Belle sat him down in front of the television and went back into the kitchen. It was slowly dawning on her what she had just done. She had only kidnapped a young boy off the street and brought him home and had left herself open to all sorts of accusations. Maybe she could keep him but that would bring all sorts of problems, what was she to do, take him back where she found him? She could never do that it was too cruel. Should she call the police but that seemed a bad idea they would throw the book at her.

She had no one to advise her, as she was still not on speaking terms with her Uncle Giles. Finally she decided painful though it was she would ask Mark

Dawson, he would know what to do but would he even speak to her?

As soon as she gave her name Mark was on the other end. "So good to hear your voice I thought you were dead."

"I have been living in Norway for three odd years but enough of that I need your advice urgently."

Belle told him what she had done and how worried she was.

"Give me your address I will be with you as soon as I can."

"I am really sorry to trouble you with this but I could not think of anyone else to ask."

"No trouble at all just sit tight I am really pleased you called me. I should be with you in about fifteen minutes."

Belle was so relieved she was sure Mark would know what to do and she was excited at the thought if seeing him again. When she looked in on Sandy he was fast asleep on the sofa. .

CHAPTER 28

Mark was with her within ten minutes, he looked a good deal thinner and he had dark shadows under his eyes not the vibrant man she had once known. That upstart of a wife of his was not looking after him properly she was thinking.

He took a look at Sandy and then came back into the kitchen.

"I didn't think, he looked so miserable and hungry now the police will think I have abducted him. How could I leave him there outside a railway station."

"Many people would have ignored him I am glad you are not one of them. There are predators hanging around these places looking for boys and girls who have run away from home for a variety of reasons. They befriend them then well, I won't go into details it is too horrific. I will make a couple of calls and we will sort it out. I sponsor a home for boys and girls mostly runaways I will ask them to come and collect the boy. He will be safe and well looked after and we will look into his background and sort things out."

Mark made his calls and gave Belle a smile.

"All sorted, I wouldn't say no to a coffee."

"Sorry I forget my manners I can't thank you enough. I won't get into trouble will I?"

"I called social services and when I gave my name they were quite happy with the arrangements I have made so you will not be going to jail, not this time anyway."

Belle laughed and handed him his coffee. "Thank you so much for sorting this out I was really worried."

"Happy I could help, you left the agency then."

"Yes it was just a stop gap, I was never happy there."

"Your talents were wasted there, you should have come and worked for me. Can I ask what you are doing now or are you married with a family?"

"No such luck I'm afraid. I set up my own photography business in Norway for over three years, did quite well actually but I got homesick and arrived back a few weeks ago. I am still into photography hope to have an exhibition one day but I am also branching out with this and that."

"You will go far you are very talented. Your advertising campaign is still running and still very successful."

"That is really good to hear especially coming from you. I never had the opportunity to say to your face how sorry I was for maligning you so I will say it now. It was disgraceful the names I called you and I never gave you the opportunity to defend yourself. You really should have taken me to court and stripped me of everything I deserved it and more. When I finally looked through my Father's papers I was shocked and mortified, misplaced loyalty of course. I did write and offer you my shares as way of an apology but you never replied."

"I did not want your shares, I wanted you. I have missed you so very much." Mark took her hand.

"Please don't do that." She withdrew her hand quickly, she wanted to throw herself at him but he was married and off limits.

"I still love you if that means anything to you."

Belle did not want to hear it she was not about to get involved with a married man no matter who he was and no matter how much she loved him.

"While you are here can I speak to you about Barnet Road, the house is ready to fall down, why?"

"No." Mark was furious she had spurned him yet again.

"You bought the house and never lived in it and you have allowed it to go into disrepair and yet you refuse to sell it. Will you sell it to me?"

"The house is not for sale and never will be. It can fall down as far as I'm concerned and the last person I would sell to is you." Mark was roaring.

"No need to shout I am not deaf. You Mark Dawson are a philistine you wouldn't know culture if it hit you in the face."

"I should have known, it had all your traits, you sent the letters about the house."

"I know nothing of any letter." Belle replied as she felt her face grow hot.

"You never could tell a lie, the letters had your stamp all over them. It seems to me all you can do is bad mouth people who do not suit in with your ideals or do what you wish, a right spoilt

brat in fact, totally heartless and a
bloody hypocrite."

"How dare you talk to me like that."

"It's about time someone faced you up
and told you what you really are."

"And you think you are the one to do
just that do you, you mealy-mouthed
reprobate."

"Can I have a biscuit Belle?"

Chapter 29

Belle tried to smile as she looked at Sandy in the doorway. "Come here sweetheart you can have all the biscuits you wish." She put the box on the table. "This is Mark he is going to make sure you are safe and well looked after."

Mark shook his hand. "How old are you Sandy?"

"Nearly eight, I hid on a train at Manchester and ended up here Mum says I get in the way too much and Uncle Raymond hits me says I am a right bugger."

"How many times have you run away?" Mark asked and took his hand.

"Three times now but I got cotched and they put me in jail. Will I be put in jail again, I didn't like it there."

"We will take you to a nice big house where there are other boys and girls just like you and we will sort everything out for you. I promise you will like it there."

"Okay Mr. Do you have a computer Belle?"

"Yes, it has games do you want to see?"
Belle took him into the lounge and set
up her laptop for him with one of the
games and went back to the kitchen.

"Am I right in thinking his Mother takes
men in and they are not nice to Sandy?"
"Yes, I'm afraid it happens a great deal,
there are many Sandy's out there."

"What I was saying before." Belle was
interrupted again as Sandy reappeared.

"Can I stay with you Belle? I promise I
will be good and make my own bed
every day and I won't be any bother
and I don't eat much."

Belle ran into the bedroom in tears with
Mark quickly following her.

"I want to keep him and he wants to
stay, what is so wrong with that?"

"The boy needs his Mother not you. He
will be placed in the home until we get
his life sorted out and he will also be
safe. You cannot give him what he
needs however well intentioned."

It was clear Mark didn't think much of
her, she could be a good mother to
Sandy if they would allow her, much
better than any home.

"I may not be much of an individual according to you but I am still better than any home you must see that. I can give him love and security."

"In this case you are not, just bloody well take my word for it."

"Don't you swear at me. You have changed and not for the better I must add, you are not the generous man I thought you were pushing little boys into homes when there are good people just desperate to look after them properly and give them the love they deserve."

"Listen to me Belle, you have no idea what you are talking about. As for how I have changed it is all down to you Belle Harcourt, I wish I had never heard the name, it has brought me nothing but bloody misery and all over a stupid little business that was not worth saving and a stuck up madam who thinks she knows everything and refuses to be bloody told. You think you know it all but I am here to tell you this time you bloody don't. There is the stupid doorbell they have arrived." Mark marched off and answered the door and he looked anything but happy.

CHAPTER 30

Belle waved good-bye to Sandy and he seemed quite happy to go with them, he was so trusting Belle thought. Mark left at the same time without even a single word to Belle and she shed a few tears when they left, it was clear Mark Dawson hated her guts now but it didn't really matter he would go back to his wife and probably tell her all about this upstart of a woman he had helped.

Four days later Belle received a typed letter from Mark informing her Sandy was back with his Mother in Manchester, she was being given a weekly allowance as long as she stopped all the boyfriends and she was being closely monitored. He also said he had given a laptop to Sandy and included her address. Sandy wishes to e-mail you from time to time. Regards Mark Dawson.

How cold it sounded, regards and it was typed. Mark Dawson could have been writing to a perfect stranger. He had certainly changed since his marriage both inside and out he was not the man she thought he was.

Belle could not resist it and she sent a reply to him.

Dear Sir, Thank you for your letter informing me re the Sandy situation.

Having met you again after three or more years I must say you have changed greatly. You sir, are a cold-hearted individual and a smart-Alec who thinks they know everything but who really knows nothing about anything. All I can say is you and that bitch of a wife of yours are well matched. As for the house in Burnet Road I will see you regret ever buying it just to allow it to rot and that is a promise and I never break my word. I thank you for your help re Sandy and if I need help in the future you will most certainly be the last person I shall ever call on, I would rather die first.

Miss B. Harcourt.

Mark smiled when he read Belle's letter. Here she was yet again maligning his character and she had her facts all wrong yet again. Dear Sir indeed, a smart-Alec and cold-hearted what was she actually saying, did she mean to start world war three? Well at least she was communicating and that was better than nothing. Tongue in cheek he sent her a reply.

Dear Miss Harcourt,

Thank you for you're most beautiful love letter it certainly made my spirits rise. I am very happy indeed to see you have changed your dictionary and not before time I hasten to add it seems the time

H B Beveridge
you spent in Norway has broadened
your education.

Yours sincerely,

Mark Dawson MBE.

CHAPTER 31

Next day Belle was busy developing the snaps she had taken of Sandy and she was really pleased with them, it also gave her a brilliant idea. She had not been allowed to keep Sandy but she could help the other Sandy's' of this world in another way which would still be very rewarding.

She contacted Sandy's mother and obtained the vital permission required when she mentioned money. She then spent a week designing an advertising campaign for the children's home and contacted Peter Latimer the person in charge.

She wined and dined him in a local hotel and set out her ideas.

"This is absolutely stupendous I am sure the money will roll in but how much will it cost we are very low on funds at the moment."

"It will cost you absolutely nothing, this is my way of helping all the children you care for a very worthy cause as I see it."

"You are a very generous lady and I am over the moon with your generosity. How soon can we get the ball rolling?"

"If you like the campaign the sooner the better, I will get the posters printed and with luck they should be circulating in a few days."

"Like, I simply love it I am sure the money will roll in just what we need at this time I thought we might need to close the home. Thank you so much."

When Belle arrived home there was a letter from Mark. She opened Mark's letter and was enraged. Love letter how on earth could he think it was a love letter. She would never ever send a love letter to a married man. He had better not tell his wife, she had no intentions of being dragged through the courts and labelled as the other woman in any divorce. When she cooled down she realised the oaf was being sarcastic. MBE they must be hard up she decided so caustically replied to the letter.

Dear Sir, Sarcasm is the lowest form of wit. MBE they must be scraping the bottom of the barrel these days or does it stand for Mean Bigoted Egotist.

B. Harcourt.

CHAPTER 32

It didn't take Mark long to see a poster and he had a huge grin on his face. He knew instantly whose work it was and it was brilliant. This would bring the donations flooding in which the home desperately needed to stay open. When he spoke to Peter Latimer he confirmed all the details and said Belle was doing it for nothing.

"She called me up out of the blue invited me to lunch and showed me her campaign. I thought she wanted paid at first but she said she wanted to help all the other Sandy's. It is fantastic, now we have two great sponsors and the money is rolling in. You two should get together what a team you would make."

My exact words thrown back in my face he wanted to tell Paul but knew that would never happen in a million years no matter how patient he was. It was clear his sweet Belinda wanted nothing to do with him and it tore his heart apart. He had waited a long time to find his partner for life and she wanted nothing to do with him and whatever he did it was always wrong. His life was not worth living if he could not be with her, all he had was work and what use was that to man or beast. He would gladly give up everything he had worked for just to be with Belle, she made him feel alive and gave him a feeling inside he could not control.

Once the posters were up parents began to call asking Belle to take their children's portraits but she turned them all down, that was not what she wanted to spend her time on. She was spending most of her time sorting through all her work and choosing the ones she felt were good enough for an exhibition, anything to keep her mind busy away from thoughts of what could never be.

One day she did something illegal. She waited outside Mark Dawson's building and when he came out she took some snaps of him without his permission. No one need ever know and she wanted it for her own personal use. The newspaper cutting from the night of the ball was small and was getting really tattered with age.

Somehow he looked quite different now, he had lost the vibrancy and energy he used to exude and he had dark shadows under his eyes. She chose the best one of the six and enlarged it then put it up on the wall of the darkroom. Every time she entered she gave Mark a kiss, not like the real thing but better than nothing and she would need to make do with that.

Peter Latimer rang Belle. "The money is pouring in and Mark has said he will match every penny whatever amount it is. You will never appreciate just what this means to us, we can help so many more children and we are planning to open a second home next year as we have the funds now. We are having a dinner dance next month to celebrate and to say a public thank you to our sponsors and also to obtain more publicity. We hope you can come as we have invited the press."

"That is most unfortunate I will be out of the country at that time."

"That is not so good as Mr Dawson cannot attend either some conference or other. That means our two biggest sponsors will be absent and I had hoped to introduce you to Mark."

"I know this is a big occasion so I will cancel my trip. I wish to help the home as much as I am able so I will attend."

"You have just made my day perfect thank you, it is really appreciated as I know what a busy lady you are. I will make sure you enjoy the evening."

CHAPTER 33

Socially Belle did not go out very much as she was on her own and the last thing she wanted was another relationship after Carl, which had been a disaster. She now knew second best was of no use to her. She decided to really go to town, hopefully her picture would be in the paper and she would show Mark's model wife she too could put on the glamour when required.

She designed a black evening gown strapless and backless, straight skirt that moulded to her every curve and a split up the side that just stopped before it became indecent. She decided to let her hair hang down but keep it off her face with two select diamond clasps she had purchased when in Norway.

When the dress was made up and she tried it on, she was not happy with the bust it seemed too low and she felt as if her breasts would pop out but she had no time for alterations so she walked around the flat in the dress to see if she ended up showing more than she should and nothing untoward happened. "Nothing to worry about there I will get away with it." she told herself.

The car drove up to the door and Peter Latimer was there to greet her. "Thank you so much for coming and you look fabulous. I have some people I would like you to meet before we go into dinner."

He took her arm and walked her through the door. Belle could see some journalists and photographers talking to some man, when the photographer moved away she saw to her consternation it was Mark, he was not supposed to be here and where was his horrible wife.

Of course this was a small charity so she would not be here, not enough publicity for her and she felt really sorry for Mark. She knew he did not like being on his own at such events. She wondered for a second if she could make some excuse and back out but knew it was much too late for that.

"Mark Dawson, Belinda Harcourt." Paul declared as he introduced them.

"We have met but it was a long time ago." Mark replied giving her a slight nod.

The papers wanted photographs so Belle and Mark had to stand together trying hard to smile for the cameras.

"Put your arm round her." Someone called and Mark reluctantly obliged.

Belle was getting more and more upset, what on earth would Mark's wife think

She never wanted to be branded the other woman who broke up a marriage.

Luckily they were not sitting together for the meal and Belle was relieved. She decided she would not wait for the dancing to begin, another appointment or some sort, any old excuse would do to get her out of here but she never got the opportunity.

Paul stood up at the end of the meal and gave a speech thanking all the sponsors big and small. He then went on to inform everyone what Belle and Mark had done personally for the home.

"We have reached a million pounds thanks to Belle's campaign and Mark has matched that amount so now we have two million pounds and the home is secure for a long time to come. We are planning another home and it will be named Bellemark as a tribute to two very generous people. I will now invite Belle and Mark to lead off the dancing."

As people applauded Belle sat frozen to her chair, she did not want to dance with him it brought back too many painful memories she just wanted out of here as quickly as possible without creating a scene if possible.

Mark cursed under his breath, he had come only because Belle would not be here, he had his photograph taken with her, had to put his arm round her, now he was expected to dance with her. Talk about rubbing salt into the wound, this was getting way past a joke he wanted to leave as quickly as possible and wished he had not come.

Finally realising he could do nothing about the situation he stood up and approached Belle and held his hand out. Belle stood up took his hand and they moved on to the dance floor. He danced her round the floor at arms length.

"You are not supposed to be here." Belle whispered.

"Neither are you."

"If I had known you would be present I would have stayed at home." Belle retorted.

"It is a great pity for all concerned you didn't do just that. You have spoilt what would have been a pleasant evening."

"Why you impudent devil, I have as much right to be here as you, you jumped up goody two-shoes. You should have stayed at home where you clearly belong as you look bloody exhausted, that wife of yours is not looking after you properly or are you so tired because

you are not getting your sleep at night,
I bet she is way too much for you?"
Belle laughed and then wondered how
on earth she could have said something
so nauseating and rude.

"You seem to know all about that type
of behaviour, just as well we are not all
like you then isn't it?" Mark glowered at
her.

"What do you mean by that remark are
you calling me a nymphomaniac?"

"If the bloody cap fits."

"Why you bloody jumped up filthy pig."
Belle bowed her head to hide her face
as it was crimson with real anger and
suddenly she felt her breasts begin to
come out of the dress.

Mark quickly held her in very close and
began to laugh hysterically. "Will I put
them back in for you?"

"No you will not everyone will see and
stop laughing like a hyena everyone is
looking at us. Trust you to think it funny
you have a warped sense of humour."

"I will take you outside and sort things
out but stay in very close to me or you
will be the spectacle of the evening,
maybe even be in the morning editions

front page I imagine or maybe even page three."

"I am in great distress here and all you can do is laugh you really are a low down rat."

"I will leave you here then and you can make your own way out, your dress is strapless and also topless now. You did say you would never accept my help again didn't you?"

"I only said that in the heat of the moment you wouldn't leave a lady in real distress would you?"

"Just try me, as you have pointed out I have changed, I am off now."

"No you can't do that" Belle clung on to Mark's arm. "Look I apologise you are not a rat but a very kind man."

"Not a smart-Alec then?"

"No of course not, please."

"How about mealy mouthed?"

No, please."

"Philistine maybe?"

"All right you win you are not a philistine or any other nasty word I used

I take it all back. Now please will you help me?"

"Not a Mean bigoted egotist?"

"Please I am begging you to help me can't you see I am in real distress here?"

"What is in for me I am a business man after all?"

"Just get me out of here and we can strike a deal you can even have my shares. Please everyone is looking at me."

"We have a deal, hang on tight to me and stay very close indeed and pretend we are glued together like lovers."

Belle was not about to argue and clung to him as if her life depended on it her face a very bright red. Mark managed to get her outside without any mishaps; he took her over to a dark corner and was about to touch her breasts.

"I can manage from here on in and you will get your bloody shares next week." Belle said angrily.

Mark took no notice his control was slipping fast. He pushed her hands away and began to fondle her breasts. Belle just gasped but did not even attempt to stop him, it was a fantastic feeling and she wanted more.

"We must get out of here Charles is round the corner I will take you home. He slipped her breasts back into the dress and Belle was bitterly disappointed. She was in no mood to argue she had made a spectacle of herself and now she had allowed a married man to fondle her breasts it was disgusting but oh how she had enjoyed it. As for the shares she could not have cared less.

CHAPTER 34

Mark after dismissing Charles for the night opened Belle's purse took out the key and opened her flat door. Once inside he began to kiss her with such passion it took her breath away. So what, he was a married man she would have him this one night and no one need ever know. She needed to find out what it was like to be with him and in any case she had lost all her wits and had to be with him just this once.

The kissing began to get frantic and Belle did not know how they managed it but they were on the bed their lips still glued together and they were undressing each other.

Mark tormented her, his hands were all over her naked body and she was pulling and tugging trying to get him closer and closer. She found his arousal and held it tight and began to guide it to where she desperately needed it but he stopped her and whispered it was too soon. By this time she was in agony she was pouring out the moisture down below and thought she could take no more.

She had dreamed of this day it was everything she thought it would be and so much more it was exquisite out of this world entirely and she was overcome with emotion. She heard herself saying she loved him and that released the floodgates, he entered her very gently at first and built up the momentum gradually until she was screaming out for the ultimate. He did not disappoint her, he drove in and got deeper and deeper till her whole being was absorbed; she had her legs wrapped around his back and was urging him on until they reached the ultimate together and it was wonderful, absolutely magical and it took her breath away completely.

It took a while for them to get their breathing back to normal and Mark was holding on to her hand in a very tight grip.

"Was it only the moment that enthralled you or did you mean it when you said you loved me?"

"Thank you for tonight it is something I will never forget. I blamed you for my Father's death, called you the vilest of names, made a fuss at the shareholders meeting then found out my Father was not the man I thought he was. I went to Norway to forget you but found out that was not possible, tried to settle for second best but found out just in time it would never have worked. I have made love with you tonight because I do love you but have broken all the rules. Go back to your wife she need never know what happened here tonight, I promise I will tell no one. I will not be the one to break up a marriage; I have made your life miserable since day one so enough is enough. Go now and we will pretend this ever happened."

"That doesn't answer my question I will repeat it, was it only the moment that captured you or was it the whole thing. Look at me when you answer?"

"I think you should leave now I have nothing more to say to you." Belle told him sharply.

"Answer my question and then I will gladly go."

"I got carried away it was just the moment, sorry."

"Look at me and say that again." Mark was not about to let it go until he was sure.

Belle looked him in the eyes steeled her heart and said in a whisper. "It was only the moment that carried me away are you happy now. Go back to your wife and you can tell her from me she is not looking after you properly."

"You never could tell a lie without your face giving you away. By the way I cannot tell my wife anything as I don't have one and you are hearing this from the horse's mouth. As always Miss Harcourt as always you have your facts very wrong but I intend to put that right with a one-off take over bid and this time there are no shares to thwart me at any future meetings."

"You married Ellen whatever her name is just after I left for Norway."

"Ellen threw me out said I was a cold fish. I could not bring myself to have sex with her or even kiss her not after kissing you. Married a shipping magnate two months later and is at this present time busy suing him for every penny she can get."

"She must be an idiot then as you are the finest man in the whole world." Belle stated with a surprised look on her face.

"Do you really think so or are you after another contract?"

"Are you sure you are not married?"

"If I were married don't you think I would know about it?"

"Then I cannot be the other woman in the divorce court."

"Assuredly not." Mark smiled and it melted her heart.

150

"Well I will tell you what I think of you and this time I have all the facts and I have checked them out thoroughly I am not wrong this time. You Mark Dawson are a fantastic, generous man and when it comes to making love you are out if this world. I love you very much and have loved you for a very long time."

"I do love it when your eyes sparkle like that, give me a kiss to seal the deal."

"What deal who mentioned any deal." Belle looked confused.

"Keep your shares and I will give you Harcourt Services and you can do what you like with it but only if you sign a marriage contract, no long engagement though, I have waited long enough but a gold band on your finger a.s.a.p."

"Then the deal is off, I don't want the company never have. However I will settle for you but it must be all of you. I want your heart and your soul. I say a resounding yes to being your wife if you make love to me again now this very minute." Belle kissed him with such passion it was a long time before they came back down to earth.

"Do you think anyone saw my breasts in that place I was mortified?"

Hostile bid

They were in hysterics when Mark said.
"Only me I think as you were clinging
on to me like a limpet but as your
breasts are so delightful I alone intend
to see them as often as possible."

Chapter 35

Belle visited her Uncle Giles intending to apologise profusely and hope she could be forgiven after all the despicable names she had called him, it was the least she could do and to be honest she had missed him since her Father died.

"There is no need for apologies Peter did not tell you the truth and of course you believed him. He fought hard to save the company but it was too far-gone. I tried to get through to him on many occasions but to no avail and when I saw how ill it was making him I had to act. I'm afraid he was a shadow of himself at the end. My only sorrow is I did not act sooner or he might still be here. I loved Peter and I know he was very proud of you and didn't wish to let you down or worry."

"You are very generous especially after the names I called you and I take every single one back and ask you to please forgive me."

"We will say no more about it and put it in the past. All I will say now is welcome back as I have missed you a great deal. I see from the papers you are engaged and to Mark. A splendid and honourable man I must add, I know he will take great care of you and you will have a very happy life together."

"To be honest I don't know what he sees in me but I am over the moon he has chosen me. I know I have a nerve to ask but will you walk me down the aisle Uncle Giles? I will understand if you say no as I treated you so shamefully."

"It will be a great honour to take your Father's place and I look forward to it."

"Thank you, now my life is perfect I have my favourite uncle back and I am about to marry the most fabulous man in the whole world and I really don't deserve it."

"Belle you are special and always will be and your loyalty cannot be faulted. Forget the past enjoy the future and you truly deserve it."

Belle was very happy she had made her peace with Uncle Giles he was all the family she had left and in lots of ways he reminded her of her Father in looks and in manner. It would be a splendid day with him by her side.

"Look what you have done now Father isn't it simply stupendous?" She told the photograph.

The wedding took place two months later and when Belle walked down the aisle on Uncle Giles's arm he whispered, "Remember what your Father said, be happy, marry and have children. He will be a proud man if he is watching you today and you are so beautiful."

Mark had waited a very long time for this day and at times it looked as if it would never happen. He was about to attain the unattainable and have the life he always dreamed of having or was he still dreaming?

He could not contain himself any longer and turned round to watch his sweet Belinda walk towards him and he thought her the most beautiful sight he had ever seen in his whole life and she was making his life perfect in every possible way. He was in heaven and the emotion completely engulfed him when suddenly he felt a searing pain and everything went black then he collapsed and fell to the floor.

Belle dropped her bouquet and ran to him. "Get an ambulance quick." She knelt down beside him tears pouring down her face trying to speak to him but he was unconscious. "Don't do this to me, wake up I need you please don't leave me alone again, Mark I need you please speak to me."

CHAPTER 36

Mark was taken to hospital and Belle sat for a long time waiting for news. She felt so alone and she feared the worst, as it was the same hospital her Father had died in. She could not contemplate losing Mark now and she cried on Uncle Giles shoulder.

Eventually a doctor came out and spoke to her. "We need to run more tests but it is definitely his heart and he clearly has not been taking care of himself for some considerable time. Stressed out I would say, in the short term we have stabilised his condition but he may need a heart by-pass. He is asking to see you and is getting into a real state, try to calm him down if you can any excitement is not good for him at this moment in time."

Belle went into the cubicle and tried to smile. "I have heard of men trying to get out of marriage but never like this."

"I need to get back to the church you must be my wife today. If I delay I know I will lose you again."

"Be sensible, once you are better we will organise another date. You frightened the life out of me I thought at first you had only fainted but you are really ill."

"We must marry now today, I cannot risk everything now, I am going to discharge myself. Please get me out of here if I wait I know I will lose you and it will be forever this time and I cannot face life without you. Please I beg of you get my clothes and get me out of here."

"You can't do that there is something wrong with your heart you must stay here and allow them to find out what is wrong and put it right."

"I lost you for many years and my life was a misery I cannot go through that again, I know you will disappear you don't want an invalid for a husband you will run off for good this time. Please, you must understand I need to get out of here now, before it is too late."

Belle was becoming more and more upset as Mark tried to take out all the electrodes they had wired him up with.

"Look at me Mark, do you love me?" Belle asked.

Mark gripped her hand tightly. "I don't care if I lose everything as long as I have you beside me that is all that matters to me, I love you more than life itself."

"I promise you will never lose me, promise me you will stay here for the next twenty-four hours at least and I will show you just how much I really love you. I don't care if you are an invalid I need you by my side or my life would be unbearable. Do we have a deal?"

"If you promise to stay with me."

"I must go and change but I promise I will be back very soon, now try to sleep it will help you, you have been neglecting yourself and I will not tolerate it, now you have your orders so sleep."

Belle held his hand gently speaking to him and stayed with him until he fell asleep then hurried away, she had a great deal to organise and she only had twenty-four hours to achieve it but achieve it she must.

CHAPTER 37

Belle called a great many people and called in a few favours as well but she was pleased with herself when she went back to the hospital and sat all night with Mark, which seemed to calm him. Next afternoon the clergyman arrived and Mark and she were married.

"Now, will you do what the doctors tell you? I do not wish to become a widow I have waited too long for you to run out on me?"

"I love you Mrs. Dawson and yes I will do what I am told I am the happiest man on earth now we are together for eternity. I will be good and I will get better very soon I promise."

"I don't care how bloody long it takes you just get better and from now on I will watch every move you make and make sure you stay healthy. I will take care of business until that time."

Mark had a heart valve replacement and although he would take a few weeks to convalesce he seemed to be making progress as long as Belle was around. The day finally arrived when he was pronounced fit enough to leave the hospital. They stayed at the hotel as the house was still being renovated and Mark's head was full of plans.

"I will take you anywhere you wish to go but first I want to spend the first few days as man and wife at my cottage in Devon. My Father died when I was only eight. My Mother could not live without a man so had a continual stream of boyfriends. Some would give me money to disappear others used their fists. I ran away four times in all. The fourth time I met Susan Dawson, she took pity on me and took me in and showered me with love. Look around and you will find some of the most neglected children simply adore their horrible mothers. I also adored my mother and wanted her to love me. Susan showered me with love but it was not enough for me and I went back to my Mother's a few months later hoping she would show me some affection, I was desperate for my Mother's love not Susan's. I went back to be with her but she did not want me and said I was a pest and was unhappy I had come back. It was then I realised just what Susan had given me. I went back and she brought me up and in the end to me she was my Mother in every respect and I took her name. When Susan died she left me her cottage and some money. I will never sell the cottage but with her money I bought an ailing company that manufactured nails and turned it round into a success and never looked back as the saying goes. I have wealth but I like to remember

when I had very little that is why the
charities I support are very important to
me. I like to think I am giving back just
a little for my good fortune."

"You are a splendid man and I love you
so very much, why you love me is a
complete mystery I am not a nice
person and when I am angry I use foul
language." Belle began to cry. "I
thought you had died just like father
and I knew I could not go on without
you, my life is with you always will be."

Mark held her close and rubbed his chin
in her hair. "I am sorry I ruined your
beautiful day, instead you had a hospital
bed. You are beautiful outside as well as
in. You are loyal to the point of being
insane. You are very talented in many
ways especially when we make love. As
for spirit there is no one to touch you
and the one thing I love the most is
your letter writing, precise and to the
point and you never miss your target.
Here is my belated wedding present to
you."

"It did not matter where or how we got
married the important part was saying I
do. I intend looking after you and no
more eighteen hour days for you and
here is my belated wedding gift to you."

"I don't wish to work again but spend my time with you and I will allow you to run the business, you are more than capable. Now open my wedding present my darling wife, I cannot wait to see your face light up."

They each opened the envelopes and started to laugh until the tears rolled down their faces, both of them had signed their Harcourt shares to each other and both were adamant they did not want them. Finally an agreement was reached they would each have half.

"Now that is what I call a real partnership, didn't I always say we would make a good team?" Mark told her.

"We will work together, that way I can take some of the load off your shoulders I don't want you to frighten me again by collapsing in a heap. You know my heart stopped in that church. Father would never allow me into the business I thought it was with me being female but of course the business was failing and he did not want me to know. You will allow me help?"

"We are a team and always will be in business and also in our personal life, you proved how valuable an asset you

are when you took charge when I was ill
and we will work together from now
on."

They spent three weeks at the cottage,
Belle loved it and she wanted Mark to
have a good rest, they spent their days
walking, talking and laughing a great
deal. At night they spent their energy
trying to outdo each other in the art of
making love. Sometimes Belle was
worried in case he was overdoing it but
was informed in no uncertain terms it
was the best medicine he could ever
have. Belle was inclined to believe him
as Mark was looking more like himself
when they got back to London and he
had also put some weight back on and
he declared he had never felt better or
happier.

"When Ellen finished with me I was
elated as I could not bring myself to
love her. I thought I would wait a short
time and approach you but you had
gone and I thought it was for good. I
did not want anything but you and in
the end I just worked every hour in the
day trying to dismiss you from my mind
but it did not work. I stopped eating
regularly well you know the rest. When
I saw you walking towards me in the
church you were so beautiful and you
were going to be mine at last, it was
just too much and my heart simply

burst. Thank you for looking after the business while I was sick you did a magnificent job, you my darling are simply fantastic in every way and I love you very much."

"What else would I do? I would do anything for you and I will see you look after yourself, I want us to have a very long married life together and I too love you very much indeed."

Belle was pleased the dark shadows were disappearing from under his eyes too. She wanted him to be healthy and stay with her forever.

CHAPTER 38

They went to view the house aa the renovations were nearly finished, the house looked marvellous again.

"I could not live in this place without you and yet I could not allow anyone else to live in it that is why I allowed it to deteriorate."

"Philistine" Belle replied then laughed.

Mark had insisted on keeping the darkroom. "You have talents you must use them but there was a most peculiar picture on one wall and it is covered in lipstick smudges."

Belle turned a bright crimson. "You didn't destroy it did you? It was the nearest thing to being with you and I got into the bad habit of kissing your picture each time I entered and I must keep it. I won't get into trouble will I?"

"Kiss me often and I will forget you ever broke the law by taking my photograph without my permission. That is a hanging offence in my book."

Mark took her out to lunch then on to an exhibition. When Belle walked in she was surprised, on the walls were her own photographs and several caricatures from way back "Where did you get all these?"

"When we took your pieces out of storage to furnish the house I found all these in a file and had an expert view them, he thought the same as I and he organised this exhibition. I also found the letter you never posted addressed to me so I opened it."

"You were never meant to see that."

"I am so glad I did. If I ever doubted your love which I don't the letter says it all. What a waste of valuable time that is the part that saddens me the most and we both made ourselves really miserable in the process."

"I thought you were married still, never mind we are together at last and making up for lost time and I could not be happier."

Suddenly she laughed when she caught sight of the caricature of Mark. "Where did you find that, I doodled that the night we had dinner to sign the agency contract I didn't know you had that it wasn't in any file?"

"The night we signed and I kissed you for the first time which to me was fatal, you dropped your purse and left this on the carpet. I thought it was brilliant and had it framed. It has been on my office wall for a very long time. I am rather fond of it."

"I will do another one with love this time."

"No, I wish to keep this one for old times sake."

As they left the exhibition Belle asked the all-important question. "Do you want children?"

Mark was thinking of Ellen, she wanted to keep her figure so children were off the agenda.

"I married you for the love I have for you, not to have children."

"So you don't want children is that what you are saying?"

"Belle I have everything I could ever want when I have you. I am not a greedy man so don't worry I will never ask you to bear my child"

"Don't you want an heir to hand everything down to?"

"What is all this about, I know we have never discussed this issue but it is really not an issue. You don't want children; I accept that so stop worrying. I will always love you come what may."

Belle kissed him in the middle of a busy street. "I want children, lots of them so it is fine if I tell you I am pregnant?"

"You are joking now, say you are joking. I cannot believe it are you really pregnant or are we speaking about the future?"

"I am pregnant now this very minute and I am delighted. You have more money than you know what to do with but I can give you something money can never buy, I can give you a real family, your own personal family."

Mark picked her up and hugged her in the middle of the street not caring who saw them.

"I, Mark Dawson am going to have his own family are you sure? I can't believe I am going to be a father and I thought I had been given everything when I had you. Oh! This is stupendous news I don't deserve all this what can I give you I must give you something." By this time the tears were running down his face.

Belle had been worried at first, now she had no doubt he wanted this baby as much as she. "You have given me your love and we have made a baby together that is all I could ever wish for now, do you think you could put me down people are staring at us."

Mark hailed a taxi, he was in a great hurry to get home and show how pleased he was with the news. He thought he had everything, but a baby it was absolutely the greatest news he had ever been given, he would have his very own family with Belle something he thought he would never attain and he need never be alone or lonely ever again.

When the taxi stopped to pick them up Belle sent it on its way.

"Why did you do that? I want to take you home quickly and show you how much I love you and I can't do it here."

"Are you feeling all right?" Belle was anxious as Mark seemed too excited and he could not stop dancing up and down.

"Never felt better, I am going to be a Dad can you believe it." Mark shouted it out loud and people were looking and smiling. One passer by even congratulated him.

"Calm down my love I don't want you to take ill again. Don't you remember Charles is waiting in the car park for us my darling? I think the news has gone to your head, goodness knows what you will be like when baby number two comes along. I intend to fill the house with our children so you had better get used to the words I am pregnant darling. What do you hope for, boy or girl?"

"I will gladly accept any gender that comes along and be truly thankful, I never dreamed I could be so fortunate in this life. I have you and now a baby I just cannot get my head round this."

"That is good, now you really must calm down as you are beginning to worry me and I no, we will need you more than ever now."

"I will calm down but only when I get you home and show you how ecstatic I really am."

"I can hardly wait" Belle replied taking him by the arm and pulling him towards the car park.

SYNOPSIS

Belinda Harcourt was a devoted and loyal daughter and was determined to annihilate the man who was responsible for her father's demise. Even after she fell in love with her enemy.

Mark Dawson was invited to make a bid for an ailing company; little did he know just what he was taking on. As soon as he met Belinda Harcourt he knew a full-scale war had just broken out.

About the author

Helen B Beveridge is a retired local government officer, she has two grown up daughters who are now independent and has finally found the time to write which has been a life-long ambition. She lives in an old mining town with her husband and apart from writing she loves gardening, baking and spending time with her family.

She hopes the reader enjoys her story and would appreciate any feedback. Helenbdepot-books@yahoo.com

Made in the USA
Charleston, SC
30 September 2012